To T

You have been an inspiration to me.

Thanks for caring!

Carol

A Different Season

F u t u r e N o v e l

Mist of the Moment

Fall 2017

A Different Season

Carol Nichols

A DIFFERENT SEASON

Nichols Now books may be ordered through Amazon.com, createspace.com or contacting:

Nichols Now Publishing at

carolnichols@live.com Or

www.adifferentseason.com Or

www.mistofthemoment.com

Cover photograph courtesy: Richard Fogg

ISBN-13: 978-0692817261

To Glen,
And the life we shared.
Thank you for each moment!

Please consider being an eye,
tissue and organ donor.

ACKNOWLEDGMENTS

With much appreciation and thanks to…

My sister, Janice Southwick, for being the first to read my manuscript and cheering me on. I love you!

Eilene Gibbens, one of my closest friends, who has spent endless hours editing. It will take more than a hug to express my gratitude. Rest up, there is a book two to be read.

Dave and Vickie Constien, for reading the beginning chapters and giving me confidence, upon completion, the book will be embraced by others. I'm grateful for your belief in me.

Linda Atkinson, for inviting me to your Thursday group that led me down this road.

Sue Pennington, Director of Bereavement, Russell-Murray Hospice, for pressing me to write through my grief and showing me I could find release through journaling.

Andrea Foster, editor/author, I applaud you for your vibrant personality, wise direction, and well-placed belief in Creative Quills writing group. You generously give to each of us your knowledge in editing, publishing, and writing. We are blessed you left life in the big city and with us now dwell.

Betty Edwards Corn, my dear friend, your help with the edit of my manuscript is appreciated more than you know and all for the price of a hug.

Dr. Shalyn Bliss, for settling the debate about stallions.

First Christian Church, El Reno, many ideas have been gleaned within your walls.

My Sunday school class, thank you for your encouragement, friendship, compassion and tender conversations.

Julie Marquardt, Cecil Nichols, and Jennifer Crowel for beta reading the manuscript, sharing your thoughts on timelines and locations.

Brett Johnson, my grandson, for technical support.

Richard Fogg, for your artistic gifts of photography and photo selection which express the essence of this novel.

Thank you to each and every one.

I try to give my imagination a few hours a day to talk to myself by placing words on paper. Hope you enjoy!

ROSIE REDMOND

Will this night ever end? Where do these stains come from? Is this a grease stain? I bet Connie isn't having this problem.

Where is she, anyway? Let's see. It's 10 P.M., so she's probably on the seventh or the eighth floor nearly halfway through her cleaning shift. Connie has the first through the fourteenth floors, and I have the fifteenth through the twenty-fourth. Then we both share the lobby and penthouse.

I'm dreading the nineteenth floor. It gives me the heebie-jeebies, remembering Mr. Ludlow's office. Did they ever give her a name? The last I remember was Jane Doe 1712, meaning she was the twelfth unidentified female body of 2017. Number twelve and all that blood. I didn't have to clean, but the sight of that night is still vivid.

The evening, by this time, has already been creepy, as Connie messages our distress text when she thinks she hears the stairwell door open. Before I can rise from the floor, she messages that she is mistaken, and then only moments later I notice Mr. Ludlow, Louis, I believe is his first name, hasn't left his door ajar. He knows all the keys I have to maneuver to unlock the offices. But wait! The door isn't locked…the knob turns, and the door partially opens. What is obstructing my entry? Trying again, I finally get the door to surrender to my persistent push. As I survey my surroundings, it's apparent the office has been—wait, there's someone--oh no! Oh no! So much blood! *Run, Rosie, run! Call for help*!

Detective Dobbins is very nice--so patient, but isn't this, after all, at least the third time I'm recounting my discovery of this horrific scene?

Finally, he's through, but I have to wait until they take my prints for comparison purposes.

What is that officer saying, "Female--maybe twenty-one or twenty-three, dressed in evening wear."

I shake my head in an effort to dispel the memories of that night, and try to return to my current job at hand, getting these stains on the floor wiped into submission. Where are they coming from?

What about the door and that note. Did I tell the young detective about the door? Oh my, I don't remember. I can't remember one day to the next what my mind is talking about.

TOP NEWS STORIES

Oklahoma City, Oklahoma (News9) Body discovered in Petroleum Tower. The cleaning crew in the Petroleum high rise discovered the body of an unidentified Caucasian female, possibly in her early twenties.

DETECTIVE DANIEL DOBBINS

"I'm not interested in hearing another word unless it begins with a numeral and ends in a street name that will lead to Louis Ludlow. Pete, come on, how hard can it be to locate someone of this high of a profile? We got absolutely nothing from that cleaning lady except hysterics. I need to revisit that whole situation with the cleaning crew after they all settle a little. Tell me what we know so far."

"We know Ludlow came from California a few months back and immediately set up shop in the Tower. We checked him through NCIC and no wants or warrants. We also checked him through the California state system."

"Anything there?"

"No, not much. Ludlow's clean except for one stop in upper Los Angeles County, but that was just a warning. He has no office personnel to speak of and seems to run a tight ship. If he needs documents dispatched, he uses a courier service. And Danny, get this! He has never been in the oil business until he turns up here in Oklahoma City!"

"Never? Are you certain?"

"Yup, seems he worked for years for some implement company out of France."

"Thanks, Pete. Hey, Pete, check with the medical examiner and see if he's got cause of death, and I want to know the results of the dead girl's toxicology screen."

CONNIE CLAIR

Oh, my. None of this is going well. I messed up when I hit my panic text to Rosie that night before I realized JJ was the one entering through the stairwell door. I'm hoping she won't remember. And to top it off, she found the note before I could get it. JJ said he had left the note on the wrong floor and wasn't able to recover it without Rosie seeing him. Wonder what the note said. When I asked him, he just said it wasn't important, and that's why he came to find me. He seemed to be visibly shaken and immediately said all was taken care of, and he would see me once I got off work.

When I applied for this job, it seemed the only way to get my foot in the door, but nothing is going according to plan. I hate the cleaning, but I did get the keys to the offices. A lot of good that did, as they gave me the wrong floors. Rosie, oh Rosie, she just had to have her way. I thought she might be an asset, but no! She kept insisting she had seniority and wanted the upper floors. She knew those floors had bigger and fewer offices per floor, so less cleaning. But that just left me out of reach of the only office I needed---the office of Louis Ludlow!

JJ said he could get us into the office before Rosie made her rounds. We just had to be patient.

JJ has been on board from the moment he entered my life. Who could ask for a better friend? And his idea seemed perfect.

Ludlow believes he's home free. Well, JJ and I don't think so. We will get everything he has taken from me. But now, finding that poor girl. Why was she there?

JEREMIAH JASON PAIGE

Can't believe how easy this is, not to mention, Connie isn’t bad looking. I’d no idea what to expect, but after our initial meeting, working my way in seemed my best option.

I thought she had ducked into the Hill Bar and Grill, and when I asked the bartender, he pointed her out to me, which went smoothly.

My initial plan was to continue following her for a while until an opportunity presented itself, but the bartender, what a dummy, nodded my way, and I’d no option but to go over.

I was taking a chance because I thought when we made eye contact at the oil building, where we both were tracking Ludlow, that she might remember me. Luckily, she showed no inkling of remembrance.

We had a few drinks, we left together, we shared a cab, and she invited me up.

Her big green eyes were so captivating, almost drawing me in, but then as they turned to sad and lonely eyes, the tears started, and the story, of which I was partly aware, came pouring out.

CONNIE CLAIR

"Oh JJ, I can still see it all when I close my eyes, the grandeur of our family estate with the pools, tennis courts and the stables. I think I miss the stables most of all, full of thoroughbreds and my beautiful Magic. Black as coal, so I named him Black Magic.

I would go and watch whenever the trainer would have him working out on the track. He was improving immensely every time he ran. The beauty of that mane and tail against his glistening coat, just needed music to go with the motion.

Charles never denied me anything."

"Wait, Charles? Is that your husband?"

"Yes, I'm Constance Sinclair, and Charles was my husband, but he passed several months ago from a brain aneurysm. We have been together from the time when we were very young. He always said from the first moment that we saw each other, across the inlet on the beautiful white beach, he knew we would be together. We were both so young, so young that we grew into life's moments hand in hand. We went to the beach and water resorts in the summer months and skiing in the winter-Aspen, Vail, and Lake Placid. And oh, the holidays! We both loved Christmas and decorating the estate was over the top with lights, lights and more lights.

His business was flexible as he was the first to have viewing parties, with large groups of cattlemen that we would wine and dine in our home. He was so intelligent and skillful. He'd make sure the buyers were comfortably seated, as the live broadcast of the cattle at the Oklahoma City Stockyards appeared on a large screen placed above our massive fireplace.

We entertained the state's royalty, the US Speaker of the House, who is from southeast Oklahoma, and the Governor and his wife. It was amusing when guests arrived, as the entrance to our estate was on the red dirt road immediately north of Northwest Highway, and until you entered the steep drive and crested the hill, you had no idea of the expanse of beauty beyond the iron gates. It was only a matter of time before the Senators and the

Governor, after much complaining of the red dust on their vehicles, had made it possible for Charles to pave our road and driveway. Also, can you imagine, the State of Oklahoma paid it all. The neighbors on the adjoining land quickly, with tongue in cheek, named the blacktop road Sinclair Boulevard.

We wanted children, but no money lavished on doctors could help with my infertility. I often watched large families in stores, large families for which it was evident; the parents could not well provide. I would turn away with thoughts of what we could give to just one child if God would so bless us. Still, even being just the two of us, we both felt complete and whole. Charles said that as long as we had each other, we could make it through anything.

The oil boom came and a substantial wave of wells appeared every half mile. I busied myself in attending, and often hosting, events for the now prosperous oil community. We welcomed to our home, the Phelps of Bartlesville, the Northrups of Ponca, the Chapmans of Enid and the Kellys of Tulsa, which at one time was the Oil Capital of the World.

At one such event, three-foot tall crystal vases were topped with large bouquets of orchids mingled with white hydrangeas, all making a resounding statement of extravagance and prosperity as the vases ran the full length of the table. Charles never wanted any centerpiece to be so obtrusive that it could interfere or hamper anyone's conversation. He agreed completely that the height of these arrangements would make for ease of eye contact and fluid speech. And that night, fluid speech was just what Charles could hardly wait to be a part of, as conversation would be hinged around a request Mr. Northrup had received from the president of J. P. Morton's Bank in New York. It seems Mr. Northrup received an invitation to join other oilmen in a symposium to address the growing concern of Arab oil companies doing business with the west. J. P. Morton, himself, seemed to think that a trust between the oil business and the bank might be in order. Of course, there would be equal numbers of trustees appointed by each member to protect everyone's interests. I must admit, I think Charles was a little envious.

Driving the countryside roads immediately to our north, a person could come to realize the many wells an owner might have as each was numbered: Wilson #1, Britington #4, Kreeton #2 and so forth.

Everyone was elated, and living the good life. Many made trips, for some, their first experience on an airplane, not to mention being in Will Rogers World Airport. Others traveled to California to see descendants of relatives that had migrated there during the dust bowl days. Some even ventured to Hawaii to celebrate a holiday or anniversary, often taking whole families and even a few ranch hands along.

Yes, the days of prosperity and abundance of cash were more than obvious. People commissioned portraits, not only of themselves but also of their thoroughbred horses.

Charles, after seeing the oil painting of our neighbors' paint horse, insisted we have one of Magic. He knew exactly where the setting would be: the spot where we always knew to look when we would return home – the knoll beyond the house where Magic would be standing in a regal posture, as if a beacon, welcoming us home.

The artist was located, commissioned, and Magic fell right into pose sensing the grandeur of the moment.

I started noticing less and less movement of the oil trucks which collected oil from the well sites. It's ironic, as I think back now. Everyone always complained of red dust being swept around by the big semi rigs but little did they realize how much they would long for that dust that would soon be no more, as wells started producing less and less oil.

Earthquakes had multiplied from four a month, a few years ago, to now well over nine hundred. Owners with damage to their homes began approaching their state officials wanting answers. The state then, on a voluntary basis, asked producers to limit the number of injection wells, as it had been suggested, but not proven, that all the waste water being forced into the Arbuckle formation through these wells was causing the seismic plates to expand, thus creating quakes that were decimating homes in the northern part of the state. With the injection wells being limited, it, in turn, dictated the number of producing wells owners could have. Therefore, a producer with fourteen wells or less would be out of business, as the cost of production could not be justified. Foreign oil then flooded the market, and soon supply and demand seemed to be in reverse.

Charles appeared unconcerned. He said a man had the capability of designing injection wells for the oil industries wastewater, and that would, without a doubt, suggest a man could still have the intelligence and foresight to present a better alternative to injection wells. Charles always thought well into the future, as he had proven before with the first virtual cattle sale a few years earlier.

The first indication of the oil impact upon us came at an event at our home with many dignitaries in attendance. It was a surprise for Charles, though, as the painting of Magic was to be unveiled.

He could hardly stand not knowing the reason for the occasion, just as much as I could hardly wait to see his face as the artist personally would be delivering and finishing the painting by signing at our home. How spectacular this would be.

We had had a scrumptious meal of Cornish Hen with cashew stuffing and prosciutto ham wrapped asparagus, prepared by Chef Chris, who often graced our palettes with delicacies he prepared in our gourmet kitchen.

The knock came at the door as we were just finishing our fruit-filled puff pastries and adjourning to the great room for coffee and drinks. My heart was beating so rapidly that I could feel my face a flush as I nodded to Charles that I would answer the door. The broad smile on his face touched my heart.

In the foyer, I snatched the gold filigree easel upon which Magic would be displayed as I greeted our kind and overly exuberant artist, Mr. Unruh.

I entered the great room and asked everyone to find a seat facing the fireplace as I entirely reduced the lighting, leaving only the fireplace illuminated. I could vaguely see Charles at the back of the room while I returned to the foyer to retrieve Mr. Unruh.

I quickly conveyed to him the magnitude of the moment and the dignitaries that were in attendance, all with baited breath. Mr. Unruh explained how excited he had been to receive my call, as he was under the impression when he last spoke with Charles, that the monies to finish the commission payment were no longer available. How elated he was that he was able to deliver the painting.

Strangely, my heart was rapidly beating, and my face a flush but for a completely different reason. What should I do; what could I do? Senators, representatives, president of the Oklahoma Cattlemen's Association, not to mention the Governor of the State of Oklahoma and Charles...Oh, Charles, my beloved husband, who had taken care of my every need were all waiting.

Now, standing so close he could feel my exhaled rapid breathing, was the artist who, with much exuberance, had said, 'No monies are immediately available;' isn't that how he had quoted Charles?

So, what to do? What could I do? There's nothing to do but lie, an outright bald-faced lie. With a deep breath and while the entire time nodding and smiling, I stated, 'Oh Mr. Unruh, that was the case, but I can now assure you, the final payment will be to you tomorrow, immediately after the bank's opening'.

I slowly looked down at my hands and run my fingers around my neck, knowing that these jeweled treasures would soon be reduced to the final payment to get sweet Magic out of hock and me out of a bald-faced lie.

The last person was gone, the staff was finishing up as Charles and I headed upstairs, up the grand staircase that any other evening would lead to the bedroom that always held so much love.

The bedroom, that was my sanctuary, where I could close the doors, lean back and know the feeling of certain bliss and confidently be secure from the outside world. The room where Charles and I could become one and know nothing could touch us or change this. Now, with every step I slowly trod, my head dropped, and my shoulders drooped in an 'oh woe is me' position.

Charles, on the other hand, seemed oblivious to the evening's events. I couldn't bring myself, during the whole charade, even to make eye contact with him. What WAS he thinking, what IS he thinking or even a better question 'Is he thinking at all'?

Our bedroom door barely shut before I said, “Is there anything I should know”?

“Know! Know what?”

"About Magic's portrait and the last commission payment? Which, by the way, I flat out lied to Mr. Unruh tonight, promising as soon as the bank opened tomorrow he would have his money."

"Oh, that. Just a little money flow problem, and I just felt I should push the delivery date."

"Mr. Unruh said you told him the final money on the painting was unavailable. That didn't sound like pushing the date."

Where was this coming from? Was this coming from my mouth? Suddenly, I just wanted to believe him and melt into his arms.

"Sweetheart, this is nothing for you to concern yourself with. I have always taken care of business, and I’ll continue to keep you in the lifestyle you so devotedly use to make our friends, and also business associates, feel loved and welcome in our home."

"Charles, you can confide in me. Here's my jewelry; take them and the others in the vault. Please take them and use them."

"Come here my love. Come here."

As he held me, I let the feeling, the feeling of complete surrender, envelop me.

The painting was hung, and I guess Mr. Unruh was compensated, as I was never contacted to the contrary.

As the following days went by, I, blissfully, and now I see, ever so naïvely, soaked up every drop of luxury, never imagining my life so quickly could change.

"Sounds like a grand life, Connie, but it's so late..." JJ states, while looking at the clock, "or I should say so early. I really better go."

“I’m so sorry, I’ve monopolized the conversation and the whole evening.”

JJ, now rising, says, “No, you haven’t. I’ve enjoyed the evening and if I'm not being too forward, I would be glad to call you tomorrow for an early dinner. Give me your cell number."

"Well...JJ, I'm afraid I don't give my number to men I have just met, and I might add, I don't even know your last name."

"You don't?"

"No, you only introduced yourself as JJ!"

"My last name is Paige, spelled with an I. Need I remind you, I'm sitting in your apartment, so your number is completely moot, don't you agree?"

"Point well taken. So, Mr. JJ Paige with an I, did your Mother just like JJ as a first and middle name, or is there more?"

"Oh, you want it all then, my full birth name!" He takes a deep breath, and says, "Jeremiah Jason Paige. My first grade teacher at school, Miss Hilton, had just admonished one mother stating that, 'Carol Sue will not be going by her nickname of Susie as only real names are spoken in my class.' Then, within a matter of days, Miss Hilton is calling me JJ. My Mother always used JJ unless I was in big trouble. I can still hear her now saying, 'Jeremiah Jason Paige, you better get over here, and I mean, now!'"

Connie can't suppress her giggle that inadvertently escapes.

"You think that's funny, do you? Well, have a good laugh!"

"No, you won't hear any giggles from me, sir, for, like your Mother, if I ever call out 'Jeremiah

Jason,' it will certainly be a heads up notice that you're in big trouble. I do love repeating every syllable though, Mr. Jeremiah Jason Paige and here's my number. An early dinner would be lovely."

"Okay, it's not like I'm not eager to continue our conversation, but only when I'm a little more rested and alert."

LOUIS LUDLOW

I've always loved the tracks. Loved the feeling of control I always received when I bet on the horses. But that day as I watched the horses in the paddock as the jockeys got ready to mount, who could have imagined that beautiful black stallion would lead me right to Charles Sinclair.

It wasn't until the moment I read his name, as I placed my bets--Black Magic? Black Magic!! I then thought of the oil site and our handshake as Charles and I named the well 'The Black Magic.'"

Shaking my head, I wonder where he is. Probably living the high life on all of my money, if I should call it my money. I tried, didn't I, to locate him.

If only I could get my hands on him. What a fool I was! I believed Sinclair would live up to his word and all on a handshake and a slap on the back.

I was so confident as I wrote out each check for startup costs. I was even elated as he conveyed that the two of us were sole owners thus making the payout even greater. The power of greed! Oh, the power of greed!

What went wrong?

I always met him at the site during delivery of the pipe and rig parts. Then, I guess, I just became complacent and too comfortable, thus trusting him more and more. The last I saw of Charles and my money was just before I had that business trip to Saveur, France. When I returned, there's no Charlie and no evidence of there ever being a well at the site. Why, oh why, didn't I stick to what I knew? Why couldn't I be content in the implement business? I still had a few months to get the money back in the proper account. I just borrowed it, right? It was just early payoff on one foreign account, so really the money wasn't legally due to the company until the close of this fiscal year.

Upon checking the Los Angeles County Clerk's office, I found a large estate owns the land, and there had been no activity in the records for years, not to mention an oil lease. Still, I thought it wouldn't hurt to check it out.

With the information received from the clerk's office, I headed up the 405, never getting tired of the drive that weaves through the mountains, the mountains that this time of year look like green velvet as the flowers began to break through heralding spring. No amount of traffic could muddy my mind with anything but their beauty.

Now passing the sprawling ranches, some being in existence prior to statehood, I watch as horses exercise, and their leisurely gait almost hypnotically drew me in. I noticed flowers, which in other states would be dwarfed, here are mammoth in size as they gallantly stretched upward to obtain every ray of sunshine for which Cali is so famous.

Why couldn't my quest to find Charles be just a pleasurable relaxing drive, ending with wine, an excellent steak, and not a mission, a fact-finding mission, to be added to my growing knowledge or better yet, my lack of knowledge of the whereabouts of Charles Sinclair?

Arriving at my destination, I was surprised to notice the quiet demeanor of the house and absence of activity compared to its surrounding area. This large of an estate would be inclined to employee numerous workers. I saw no movement in any of the outbuildings, and the stalls seemed deserted, with no recent disturbance apparent to the grounds.

I parked on the north end of the house and entered the long deep covered porch, which is common on these Spanish hacienda style homes. I glanced through the numerous windows as I approached the heavy wooden double doors. I lifted one of the large brass knockers and waited for any sound of approach. A second attempt resulted in the same silence.

I looked behind me towards the tree line, and to each end of the porch, I continued toward the south, deciding to walk the perimeter back to my vehicle. Donning my sunglasses as I exited the porch and noticing the sun scorched earth which is begging to be quenched, I walked confidently forward. As I passed the large expanse of side windows, I missed no opportunity to catch any movement, but only deathly silence prevailed. As I turned the corner to the east and backside of the house, a lazy cat halted my advance and quickly retreated with arched back and tail askew. Before me now was a large deep porch that mirrored the front, except for being enclosed in glass panels.

I met no resistance from the door, and as I checked the areas behind me, I stepped forward just as the back entry door opened revealing a petite dark-haired woman of, I'm guessing, early twenties and holding, no less, a shotgun which quickly got my attention as she racked a shell into the chamber.

"I would suggest you back up slowly and cautiously with your hands in the air and no sudden movements to give me an excuse to pull this trigger."

"Ma'am, I just want some information. I mean no harm. I've driven out here from Los Angeles looking..."

"I said, back up and continue walking that way and no talking," as she motioned with the barrel of the gun toward the direction of my car.

"Okay, little lady, I'm walking. I'm just trying to locate a gentleman by the name of..."

"I said, no talking. Move! Move!"

As I approached my car and began to enter, I turned and looked her squarely in the eyes and said, "Now, as I was saying and I'll continue, because I believe you will have a hard time explaining my body if you pull that trigger on someone half in their vehicle. I'm inquiring about Charles Sinclair."

I saw the motion in her eyebrows as one brow took a definite tilt, and her eyes seemed to glaze at the mention of his name as if she remembered some previous moment in time. Her dark hair and high cheekbones added to her beauty, but as the fierceness and contempt returned to her eyes, I was quickly reminded of my position in this situation and leaned further into my car.

She stoically stood her ground, but not deterred I continue pushing, noting the furor my words had provoked. She finally denied knowing of Sinclair, but why wasn't I buying it? With every answer, she seemed to glance away as if not being completely honest. 'No wells on this property,' is what she said. Strange wording, no wells on this property. Why not, no wells on my property. When I asked for the owner's name and whereabouts, that was the end of any further conversation. She determinedly raised the gun and encroached into my space. I cautiously entered my vehicle, but I never broke eye contact with her. If she was going to shoot, she was going to know the feeling of watching life exit a man's body at her doing.

The return drive to LA wasn't as relaxed as I'd experienced on the drive up. I just couldn't seem to keep both hands on the wheel. I kept feeling the need to rub my forehead, and as my left hand repeatedly moved lengthwise from my eyebrow to my temple, I tried to make sense of the whole situation.

I rethought what I knew for sure. I knew I met Charlie numerous times at a location that the county clerk has identified as being on the large expanse of land belonging to that address in upper Los Angeles County. Maybe they were mistaken, and why didn't I get further information? If they could give me the address, they surely could give me the owner's name. I'd recheck with the county clerk just to make sure I was correct. But no, she knew something! It was too obvious. Her action might have been appropriate with me entering her porch, and it being her back porch at that, for her to greet me with a shotgun. If her action was appropriate, her reaction was a dead giveaway. Louis, dead, watch your words as that's what you almost were-DEAD-and now you're at a dead end.

A night's sleep and then I'd hit the trail tomorrow.

Wish I could have gotten more out of the girl in upper Los Angeles County.

I revisited the restaurants and bars where we had eaten, but all is futile as, everyone remembered us but knew nothing more of Charlie than I currently did. Another dead end. With every tick of the clock, my fate was moving closer to that of an embezzler looking at jail time.

Now, here at the tracks on the betting sheet, I saw the name Black Magic. Could this be more than a coincidence? Could this be an omen of things to come?

I quickly forgot placing my bet as the only betting I was doing right now was in my head, yes, betting I might have a lead on that cheating Charles Sinclair.

I thought a visit to the stables was in order.

I knew it, I knew it...someone is looking out for me. Black Magic's stall was in the entrants' stables, so he wasn't permanently boarded there. The temporary placard said the owner is C. Sinclair, Remington Park, Oklahoma. That had to be Charles Sinclair, but Oklahoma? That made sense. I should have thought of that myself, to check the other states that are big producers of oil.

I hurried out of there before the races were over. I wanted to have the upper hand when Charles Sinclair showed up at the stable, and then we would see what he had to say for himself.

I heard the start of the race in which Magic was running, as I was watching one of the many live monitors. I thought, not too bad, fast out of the gate, but he had a mile and a quarter to hang in there. It didn't matter if he won or lost because I was going to be the big winner at Santa Anita that day, and it didn't cost me a penny. Thank you, Lord, it was just March, and I still had three months until year-end when the accounts had to be back in balance.

Ducking into the closest building, I waited for the returning horses. There he was, that black beauty, his trainer and some well-dressed blonde woman who was slender, tall and very, very attractive. The way she was making over that horse, she should know something that will add to my good fortune of this day. Still no sight of Sinclair as I decided to go over.

“Beautiful horse, he ran great today."

"Thank you, we're very impressed with him, and our trainer is pretty proud of what stamina and heart he has shown. I'm sorry, this is our trainer, Doug Hartly, and you are?"

"Oh, I'm just a horse lover from way back, and this is one beautiful black horse. And what a very well fitting name, Black Magic."

"Yes, my husband gave him to me, and I'm completely and unashamedly enamored with him."

"The placard said the owner is C. Sinclair so C. Sinclair is your husband?"

"Yes, well no, not exactly. I'm the owner. I'm Constance Sinclair, but my husband and I share the same first initial as his name is Charles."

"So you and your husband are here on a little racing trip. Where is your next race?"

"A couple more in state, then final at Remington. Of course, we leave all of that up to Doug."

"You and your husband should take in a little of the nightlife while you're in our beautiful state."

Come on, lady. Come on, give me something here. Where is that so and so...?

"Oh, Charles doesn't do the race circuit. He's far too busy to take an interest in racing, but he often tells me what makes me happy always makes him happy. He's such a sweetheart."

"Yes, a sweetheart. I'm certain I would agree if I knew him as you do. Good luck on your next race."

"Sir, I'm sorry, I didn't catch your name."

Walking away, "I guess not, but as pretty as you are, I certainly will remember Constance Sinclair and Black Magic from Oklahoma."

JEREMIAH JASON PAIGE

Amanda had told me that a man had come to the house asking questions concerning her father. I found her in the swing on the front porch holding the shotgun. She was so shaken by the experience she could hardly sit long enough to speak. Then while pacing the length of the porch, she finally got to the part where she finds out the stranger's name. She had no idea who the stranger could be until Dwayne from the Sheriff's Office pulled in and asked if everything was okay, as he'd stopped a car speeding from our drive. The deputy said he'd issued him a warning, and after she inquired, the deputy stated his name was Louis Ludlow and was from Los Angeles. Said Ludlow had told him he was an implement sales representative and was out here on business.

"Just call him! Just call your father."

"No, Uncle JJ, no, I can't, and quit calling Charles Sinclair my father.

"Amanda, you just have to get over those feelings. You need to just call him and see if you're in any danger."

"What danger? Just a man asking questions."

Laughing and now standing looking out the front toward the main entrance, JJ comments, "Just a man that took far too many liberties by looking in windows while walking the entire perimeter of the house. No, you're right, I see nothing wrong with that, and if it was no problem, and you didn't feel a little threatened, why did you deem it necessary to load a shell into the chamber of the shotgun?"

Glancing her way, and seeing Amanda had disconnected from the conversation, he continued, "What is it, what's on your mind?"

"I knew it; I had a feeling Charlie was close. I thought I saw him one day, not long ago. Besides, he never cared for us, and I didn't even know he was my father until after mother became ill."

"But you liked him before you knew who he was. You adored him when you were younger. The moment he drove up you would run hollering,

‘Charlie, Charlie. Momma, Charlie's here.’ You followed his every step, tugging at him until he picked you up and threw you in the air making you squeal with delight."

"Uncle JJ, I can't, after all the things that have been said between us."

"Listen, Amanda, I didn't like him either when your Momma took up with him, but what could I do? She was a grown woman, and I was only her kid brother. She met him when he was out checking on his family’s land. She knew he was married, but she didn’t seem to care, and she wouldn’t listen to a word I said. Her face would light up every time he came, and upon his leaving, she just calmly waited for his next return. You’re living where your father’s momma came during the glory days while her husband stayed in Nevada and worked the rails sending money to obtain all this land. He took care of you and your Momma, and you never wanted for a thing and still don’t.”

Amanda still pacing, "But then he was gone. I said all those terrible, horrible and demeaning things, and he just turned and left."

"He might have left, but he still made sure that no one can ever take this land from you. I'm confident that he would have continued his visits, after giving you a little time to process, knowing your whole life had been a lie, if only you would have given him the tiniest window of opportunity."

"Uncle JJ, what to do, oh, what to do?"

LOUIS LUDLOW

Upon locating the palatial estate just west of Oklahoma City on Northwest Highway, I was surprised but grateful, the massive gates with the larger than life monogrammed S were not obstructing my entry. *That's an open invitation to visit, correct? Yes, I'm going in.*

Five car garage but no cars in the portico, so is he here or isn't he? The front door glasses are opaque, so I can't see beyond.

Wonder if there's an alarm? I would imagine. This place has to be filled with a plethora of items bought by the quite, quite wealthy owners.

Manicured flower beds, box cut shrubs, stately trees and big hydrangea bushes stand as if guards on each side of the large porch.

The south side of the home is banked with large windows happily receiving the sun. The back opens to a raised patio with an attached loggia and full open air kitchen, which sets to the north end of the area. Every entrance has double French doors with windows to each side, which allow the view of the gardens that extend forever, or so it seems.

Trying the second set of French doors, I surprisingly enter the unlocked garden room. I'm almost inclined to stop and smell the many live orchids, each displayed before a grand mirror, doubling their beauty.

Come on, Louie, remember the task at hand. Just find his office, get what you need on the flash drive, and get out of here.

A shining marble floor greets me as soon as I enter the adjoining room, a dining room with a table that could seat twenty people easily is to the right of the main entry. To the left is what seems to be a morning room, all in yellow and peach. Straight ahead, yes, straight ahead, Wow, oh wowzer.

Have I ever been in a room this great with any higher beamed ceilings than this? If I have, it was a church; yes, the church in Saveur, France. *Oh Lord, I felt so close to you there. What am I doing, Lord? I can't do this. This isn't the way.* I'm almost to tears and shaking as I illegally stand in another man's home, another man's sanctuary. As I slowly back, retracing my steps, June 30 pops to the forefront of my mind. The money has to be back in the account by year-end. Either way, leave here and go to jail for fiduciary fraud of funds entrusted to me or continue and risk being caught as an intruder and be immediately taken to jail. Yes, those were my only options.

I spur myself forward as I harden my heart further to any memory of the lofty cathedral in France and any redemption for me.

I find the office but no computer or laptop. I check every desk drawer, and the credenza turns up nothing. Maybe I'll just wait for him to return, and see if we can work something out. Surely, Charles will be willing to give me a partial return on my money, and I can get that back into the company. Or not? Yes, I'm certain his decision will be, or not, because he went to great lengths to disappear.

My assistant, Cassie, didn't realize what a gift her sudden departure for another job has turned out to be, forcing me to jump in and learn more of the clerical part of the company. I was very agitated when she quit before my France trip, and period-end reports were due. She handed me her flash drive and said, 'Everything off my laptop is on here.' When she began to explain further, the magnitude of this little device opened an entirely new world. A world that will bring Charles Sinclair to his knees and make me whole. Isn't that what they say in court cases, the defendant is requesting the court to find in his favor and order the plaintiff to make the defendant whole again? But I want whole and punitive damages also. I'm fed up, I'm mad, I'm livid!! You just wait. Big Boy Sinclair will no longer be because I'm bringing you to your knees.

Louis, get on with it. Where next? That only leaves upstairs as I lift my eyes to the grand staircase leading to the next place to search.

I see it! The computer is on the desk in the master bedroom. Now where is that flash drive? Turn this baby on, get it all transferred, and get out of here. ENTER PASSWORD. Password! Surely, he has that written somewhere. I rifle through the drawers but find nothing. I have mine on a sticky note under my desktop calendar. Could it be? Yes!

A pink sticky note. Pink. Whatever. Oh my, there are several written down. Well, I'll start at the top and work through. The computer is blinking. I only have one more try before being locked out for two hours, but I have two passwords left. Eeny Meeny, I'm going with this one. Yes! I'm in!

Calculating time to download file manager programs. Come on, come on, just do it!

Now looking out the oversized window of the alcove, I don't see anyone near the house, but the estate seems quite busy with workers everywhere out back. The view is quite beautiful of the lakes, and you can even see the distant city off to the east.

There's the tone alerting me it's loaded and done. Yank this baby free, and get the heck out of here before any of the estate help sees me.

Too late! Someone is approaching.

"What are you doing here? Who let you in?"

When exactly did I cross that line when everything went so horribly wrong? *Think Louis! How can I ever explain being alone and upstairs? Charles will surely and very quickly determine I have been through his desk. And his computer, oh no! I left his laptop open and still on!*

I begin to speak with him with trembling demeanor, then…

"I just wanted a date, some proximity to a time when I might recoup some of my investment." I should have controlled my breathing better, but my heart was pounding, and sweat beaded my brow.

But Charles just laughs that big robust laugh that so easily endeared him to everyone he met and made it so easy, too easy even, to embrace his ventures, as he pushes me for a plausible reason to be alone upstairs in his home.

With every question from Charles, the more I become entrapped and feeling unable to find a way, any way to escape this situation without being found an intruder, an illegal intruder. What could I possibly say that would be viewed credibly?

In the blink of an eye, as his voice rings through my head with echoes of thundering accusations, I push him, and down the grand staircase he tumbles until reaching the marble landing below.

As I hear someone entering the downstairs door, I quickly retreat through the back stairway, praying I will see no one, and none of the staff will see me.

CONSTANCE SINCLAIR

"Charles, Charles, oh Lord! Let him be alive!"

The ambulance is here, and I'm to follow them to St. Anne's, yes, meet them there.

I hate the waiting, but his fall was so precarious. What could have happened?

I thought someone was there with him...the car in the portico, was it blue or maybe gray?

When I shouted for help, Consuela was the only one that came. Then as the EMTs loaded Charles into the ambulance, it was parked in the exact spot I'd seen that car. I wonder...

"Mrs. Sinclair, your husband's fall caused swelling in his brain, and it's imperative that we relieve the pressure. He is being taken to the operating room for the procedure. Could you please sign these consent forms?"

"Of course, of course! Can I see him? Please, I need to see him."

"I'm sorry, but they have already taken him to surgery and are waiting for my call advising of your consent before they begin. Wait here, and I'll show you to the consultation room where your husband's surgeon will meet with you after the procedure."

OR Consultation Room for immediate family only. Might as well have said, 'For his only living family.' I'm it, his immediate and only family.

Oh Lord, I'm on my knees lifting my husband up to you. Guide the surgeon's hands, so he may have the skill needed to get Charles back to me. I need your peace, Lord. Wrap your arms around me, and give me the peace to know that you're in control. We love you, Lord, and give you all the praise and glory. In the name of Jesus, Amen.

Why didn't I ask how long? How long has it been? I forgot to check the time. Oh, Lord.

"Mrs. Sinclair, I'm Dr. Lang. I'm one of the neurosurgeons at St. Anne's, and I have just come from performing the procedure on Mr. Sinclair. My intention was to relieve the pressure and possibly stem the bleeding in the brain. I was able to stop the bleeding."

"Doctor, that's wonderful! Thank you so much."

"No, Mrs. Sinclair, I wasn't quite finished. I was able to stop the bleeding, but Mr. Sinclair has another aneurysm which needs to be treated by a procedure known as endovascular coiling."

In a slowly exhaled breath, "Another aneurysm?"

"Please, Mrs. Sinclair, let's sit here. Yes, right now there are only a few hospitals that have specialists with surgical equipment to do this very technical and delicate procedure. I'll be in contact with one, or both, that are in our proximity, and we will go from there. I'm sending him by Med-a-flight."

Staring at her hands, "Thank you, Dr. Lang."

Suddenly rising, “Doctor, Doctor, may I see him? May I see Charles? Please, I need to see him!”

"Someone will come for you as soon as your husband is in recovery, but I’m not certain of his abilities to communicate at this time."

"He won't even know I'm there? He won’t even know I’m with him?”

"I didn't say that, Mrs. Sinclair. We believe that the patient is able to recognize a loved one’s voice, and we encourage conversation with them."

"Thank you, doctor."

Oh Lord, Dr. Lang has left me so much to think about, alone in this quiet, still room. I don't like it when the silence comes, and I'm left with only my thoughts.

ROSIE REDMOND

Well, I'm here, the nineteenth floor. I'm not starting in Ludlow's office; besides after the initial cleaning, it usually needs little done.

Is that another spot? Yes. This is impossible. Looks like the same spot I have been toiling over in front of the stairwell door on eighteen.

Where are my keys? Here they are, and what is this? That note. That note I found on the stairwell door. I have been rolling it back and forth in my head whether to bother the young detective or not. He did ask if I'd noticed anything unusual, hadn't he? I wonder who was supposed to get this. It is only three words all in capital letters with an exclamation point. DON'T COME UP! Don't come up? Don't come up where? And being on the stairwell door that means for whoever it was intended would be using the stairs and not the elevator.

Wait, hadn't Connie's distress message said something about hearing the stairwell door open? Where's my phone? It should still be on there. Yes, here's the first message she texted using our distress code at 10:12 P.M. then at 10:13 P.M., she said, 'I thought I heard the stairwell door, but I was mistaken.' That's only a minute's difference in the time. How could she possibly be that certain it was nobody in a minute's time?

Should I ask her or just forget it? What about Detective Dobbins?

I can't worry over this now, as I'd better get to this spot. I wonder if they have been moving any office furnishings or equipment. I bet that's it. It's grease from a roller on the equipment or the transportation cart.

LOUIS LUDLOW

Back to safety. Back home from Oklahoma with this flash drive after downloading all of Charles Sinclair's computer files. Now, let's see if I can remember exactly how Cassie had instructed me to transfer the files to my computer.

Oh, wow, this isn’t going well. No program found to open file. Let's try another one. Same result. No program found.

I think I've done everything correctly. Why didn't I write it down? Should be the same as I did when she gave me her computer's flash drive. Let's just give her a call. Never thought I would be calling a competitor of ours for assistance, but it's just Cassie, and she won't mind.

She said I shouldn't have to select a program as both of our laptops were identical, and her files she had on the flash would just automatically know what program to use to open. Now, what do I do?

I had to do a lot of talking to convince her to help me, and finally, she said, "Just send me the files, and I'll open and send them back."

CASSIE WALTERS

"Thanks, Louis, I got the files. I'll speak with you later to let you know when I have them converted and open."

Let's get these opened, and see if this possibly is something I can use to my advantage at my new job. What is this? Oil specs at different well sites in Oklahoma and formulas for oil, gas and waste separation. This looks interesting; I might keep a copy. Louis will be none the wiser. I wonder, is his implement company going to venture into equipment for oil sites?

"Hello, Cassie. I received your email and was able to open the attachments. I owe you big time."

"No problem, Louis. We worked together for too many years not to still be friends, even though I'm with a different company now."

After hanging up, *that's right, Louis, too many years not to know you're up to something. I'll just keep this in my back pocket, and bide my time.*

LOUIS LUDLOW

Okay, let's see what we have now. I need to research and study these specs before I can calculate what exactly Charles' idea is and what direction will be appropriate.

I think we have made a fair trade, Charlie, your computer files in lieu of my money. Deal? Deal!

All these weeks and I'm right back at the same conclusion, I need samples from the wells themselves, before I can move from theory and reach the final results. A result which I believe will be the answer to removing injection wells from oil sites. Charlie, you were truly a forward thinker. These plans for an evaporative system that just leaves salt as residue is ingenious. This system will remove the need to have injection wells that send the wastewater into the Arbuckle formation. That's exactly what the geologist at the USGS Federal Earthquake Center believes is causing the Oklahoma earthquakes that occur daily. Cha Ching!!

CONSTANCE SINCLAIR

“Thank you all so much for coming. Charles would have been touched if he had only known the outpouring of his friends’ celebrating his life. I count each of you as a friend, even though I have only met some of you through Charles as his business associate. I know the seating was limited at our small church but, I just had to have Charles’ funeral in the same location that we were married. Thank you for understanding and indulging me.”

Upon leaving, my close friend hugged me and said, "Connie, please call. We are so close, anytime you need to talk just call me."

"Thank you, Geri. This has been such a roller coaster from the time I spoke with Dr. Lang in the OR consultation room to the flight to Ketter White in Dallas. Charles didn't even make it to surgery. They just pushed me out of the room as the doctor said I needed to leave.

Geri, I just fell against the wall and said, 'Please Lord, I'm here alone, and they said don't worry. Oh Lord, we thank you for every positive moment where Charles can draw a breath.'

We have shared every second of life hand in hand, Geri, and that's exactly how it ended. I entered the room and seeing all the tubes and hoses attached, I took his hand and said, Thank you for being my husband, I'm so blessed to be in your life."

Geri says, during tearful embraces, "Well, please know I'm just the next section up and don't hesitate to call if you think of anything."

With the door now shut, I began talking. Yes, I was talking, but to no one, yet I was talking to the life of which I no longer had control and ill equipped to handle.

LOUIS LUDLOW

I, fortunately, was able to obtain an office in the Oklahoma City Petroleum building. Or maybe I've chosen the wrong word, as fortunate might not be correct. Don't know if that is fortunate or not, but time will tell.

I think I have everything I need to obtain samples. If the internet query is accurate, one gallon from each site will be ample. Got the locations in my GPS. Now to get this ball rolling.

I obtained the samples from all six wells, but what can I use to transport to my office? I'll stop at Target and get their largest piece of luggage. Here's hoping I can make it in one trip and not two. I don't want to draw any attention that will lead to questions like, *"What could you possibly need with a piece of luggage that big? Are you taking an international cruise?"*

All loaded, and as luck would have it, the oil samples just fit. Almost there, and the elevator has yet to stop and take on another passenger. One more floor, but as the door opens, there are numerous people leaving the conference room across and down the hall. I am nervous over one person seeing this behemoth suitcase, but I certainly don't want twenty seeing it. "*Think, Louis! Go down a floor, and get off. Hurry, close the door.*"

Good, looks like the coast is clear on eighteen. Do I wait? No, too many people, the elevator will be congested for quite a while. I'll take the stairs. Oh, my word, half way up, and I'm out of breath. Even using both hands, I can only manage to maneuver one step at a time.

Finally in! Bolt the door, and louver the blinds. Now, get this in the locked file room that's in the far end of the closet. Geez, There is so much stuff stacked in front of it, but you know, that just might be a good thing. I'll put everything back.

Done! Now I'll wait until after closing and before the cleaning shift gets to my floor to do anything further.

Where are some paper towels? It looks like one of the canisters is leaking. It's left a spot from where it was sitting. It isn't very large, but I don't want to give that nosy cleaning lady anything which she can blab to others. I see where she moves things on my desk. I wouldn't even put it past her to be eating from my snack drawer.

CONSTANCE SINCLAIR

I have seen that car before! Yes! It's the same car from the portico that day I found Charles at the foot of the staircase.

I can't believe I've forgotten. But, no wonder, my life has been a whirlwind from that horrible day to this very moment. Get in the house and to the bedroom and see if I can see if the car turns in at a neighbor's. Though, I don't remember any of our neighbors having a gray car.

Where are Charles' binoculars? The car is at one of our well sites. Should I go and confront him? No, get a tag number!

"Thank you so much, Grant. That was speedy. I knew you would be able to get me the information on that tag. But no name, just that it's a rental? Oh, Grant, that's fantastic! You did get a name, Louis Ludlow."

Now what to do. How can I figure this out? Maybe I should make a trip to Enid and enlist the help of Phillip. He's a good friend, and he has been at all the gatherings here that had to do with oil. It's still early morning, so I'll call now and see if he's available.

"Phillip Chapman, please. Yes, this is Constance Sinclair."

"Hello Connie, how are you doing? Joyce and I are both worried and concerned, but didn't want to intrude."

"I was wondering if you would be available to see me if I started to your office right now?"

"Certainly, come on up. I've wanted to speak with you concerning Charles and a venture that he was pursuing."

As I crest the knoll and wait as the gates swing open before leaving the estate, the gray car carrying Ludlow speeds toward Northwest Highway, and I, without further consideration or forethought, fall in behind, though at a safe distance. “Been visiting more of our oil sites, Mr. Ludlow? I know you were with Charles the day of his fatal fall, and I have you in my sight now.”

Ludlow turns east onto Northwest Highway toward Oklahoma City.

“Why were you there? What did you want from us, or what did you want from Charles? I haven't noticed anything missing, but if you needed something from Charles, it would be oil related.”

He’s turning into the Petroleum Tower Office Plaza. Wonder who he’s seeing there?

Hurry, Connie, so you can tell on which floor he will be exiting.

One of the security guards quickly blocks my entry. "Ma'am, you need to sign in and please enter the name of the business you’re visiting. I’ll call to let them know you’re on your way up."

"Oh, I just need to see your directory, please."

Nodding to Connie’s right, he states, "It's on that carousel."

Turning, I awkwardly run into the gentlemen immediately behind me. "Please forgive me."

"No problem, my fault entirely."

Why didn't I pretend to sign and then see what business he wrote down to gain entry?

As I scan the directory, I continue to watch the bank of elevators to see upon which floor they stop, but there are too many stops to give me hope of locating what office Ludlow is visiting. If I could only come up with some way to get past the guards.

Let me go back, sign in for one of these businesses, and check the names above me for Ludlow.

"Yes, Sir! Sir! I'm ready to sign in."

"Okay, here you go, ma'am."

Connie perusing the list, “What? No Ludlow. He didn't sign, as the only names listed in the last thirty minutes are two ladies.”

Let me check the directory once more. I must recognize some of these names, as every oilman in Oklahoma has been to at least one dinner we hosted, I'm sure.

No. No. No! I don't recognize that name, but these are company names and not personal names except Ludlow, LLC. He has a business here! No wonder he got through check-in so quickly.

"Ma'am, ma'am, you need to sign in, or I must ask you to leave."

Turning to leave, Connie high-hats the guard. "Leave, huh, who needs three guards at one entrance anyway?"

I think my visit to Enid to see Phillip is more pertinent than ever. He surely can shed some light on this gentleman or know something of his oil ventures.

"Constance, do come in. My deepest condolences to you."

"Thank you, Phillip. You and Joyce have been so kind, and the floral arrangement was beautiful. I have nothing but sweet memories, even though it seems our life together went so quickly."

"I'm so glad you called because I wanted to speak with you but didn't want to intrude on your grief."

"I'm okay, Phillip; I was just blessed to be in his life."

"I wanted to make sure you were aware that Charles is, I'm sorry, was in the process of developing an evaporative system to handle waste water for the gas and oil industry that's going to be monumental. He was rushing it through when he came into his financial problems and had to slow a little until he could obtain more backing."

"Financial problems?"

"Oh, Connie, I thought you were aware. Hasn't Charles' attorneys gotten with you?"

Shaking my head weakly, as if recovering from a sharp slap to the face, I raise my eyes to meet his gaze, and where a moment ago his eyes were active and alive, now they show nothing but pity. I shiver, as I'm taken aback, realizing I have never been the object of pity from another human being. "*Could my circumstances be that dire? How bad are they?*"

"Phillip, you must excuse me. It was good of you to see me." All the while, I'm smiling and nodding as I quickly exit, knowing I have to find the air, find the sun, find…Oh Lord…find which way to turn!

The entire drive home, I feel deathly ill, believing any moment I must pull over and retch. Retch every ounce of grief, retch every ounce of fear, retch every ounce of facing the unknown, facing the next turn in the road, or is it off a cliff? "Oh Lord, I can't find a day, an hour, or a minute I don't feel devastated and alone."

I must get home! I must get to security where I can shut the world out and think.

I drag myself, as I heavily lean into the banister, up each stair, each step taken forcefully brings back, in rapid flow, what I've faced all these months. Shutting my bedroom door, I slide to the floor with this final prayer: *"Lord, I need to forget, just for a little while, I need to forget,"* as the flood of tears, mixed with sheer agony, take control.

The sun wakes me as I glance at the clock. I realize I've slept well into the middle of the afternoon. The rays glistening on the garden, as I roll over and gaze out the doors, makes me stretch and yawn as I slowly return to the reality of my life.

Charles, how could you have done this to me, to us? You just stayed so busy taking care of us, and I just stayed so busy making you happy and loving you with all my heart and soul. You were always supportive, and I counted on you so much. You believed in me and let me pursue my own venues. It seemed you were always there at the exact moment I had a problem or ran into a roadblock. You were never obtrusive. You could be found on any of my journeys. Yes, you could be found on the way but never in the way. As the days go by, sometimes I miss you so much, it's hard to breathe remembering the moments, our moments.

Now, I have been informed, but not formally of yet, by Phillip that I'm destitute or close to it. What was his exact wording? "I wanted to make sure you were aware that Charles is, I'm sorry, was in the process of developing something for the gas and oil industry that's going to be monumental. He was rushing it through when he came into his financial problems and had to slow a little until he could obtain more backing."

That's why Charles went to California for that extended stay, wasn't it? He said he had to be available to answer clients' questions and any concerns with startup cost for something or the other. Why didn't I pay more attention? I just was unhappy, because he was spending the winter months in the sun, while I stayed home through an Oklahoma winter. I told him he would have to go back with me in March to see Magic race if he wasn't still out there at that time.

If he was developing something for the oil and gas industry...

Leaping from bed...Quick, where is Charles' laptop? Yes, it's on the bedroom desk in the alcove. Turning it on, I reach for the passwords which are under the desk calendar, but no passwords. I throw the calendar, pens, and paperweight to the floor in a mad search for the pink sticky note that had always been under the right side of the calendar. Opening all the drawers, I still find nothing that even slightly resembles a sticky note. As I exhale and lean back in the chair, I see the wastebasket and a wadded piece of pink scrap paper torn in half. I piece the torn note back together and enter the first password. With shaking hands, I enter the password to open File Manager and the computer programs, so that I can see the contents of each folder. I tap on the first yellow file, and nothing opens. I frantically continue with each additional folder, all with the same results. Nothing! Again nothing at all on an evaporative system. All gone. Leaning back, enveloped in the soft leather of Charles' desk chair, I say, "Charles, now I know who caused the fall that took your life, and I also know what you, more than likely, caught him stealing."

I glance out the French doors, only this time, I have the view of the distant city where Louis Ludlow has, oh so confidently, opened his business. *"We will just have to see about that; we will just have to see..."*

JEREMIAH JASON PAIGE

"Connie, you look very nice."

"Thank you, kind Sir."

"Thank you for gracing me with your presence for dinner." Then with a raised eyebrow, JJ repeats, "I must say you look very fetching."

"Fetching, huh. I have been the recipient of many compliments, but fetching is a first for me."

"Shall we order?" Then after a pause, "I'm afraid the drink menu here will be very limited."

"Please, you may order for us."

As the waitress removes their plates and leaves the check, Connie says, "The dinner was delightful, but I would've been fine with going Dutch treat."

"I know, more of that modern day, 'I am woman, see me roar,' right? But from the conversation, during our chance encounter last evening, I have the feeling you're more accustomed to being on the receiving end than picking up the check end. Your face was priceless when we stopped in front of this diner. No white cloths or white tie and black-coated waiters. Just Lucy with her 'What cha' havin' folks? The meatloaf or liver and onions are both good.'"

With reddening face, "I was hoping it wasn't that obvious, and I do believe that's the first time I've ever eaten meatloaf. Exactly what 'meats' are in meatloaf, or do I want to know?"

Now, with his chuckles ending, he continues, "Oh, it's just ground up meat parts, but I bet you use that as dog food."

Glancing at her hand, she rubs the soft still-lined area where her wedding set should be, and JJ suddenly sees the return of the saddened green eyes that are so hard not to race to comfort.

"Do you want to tell me more? Are you comfortable with continuing?"

Connie nods assent and continuing, cries softly as she recounts finding Charles on the landing at the bottom of the grand staircase. She reaches for another tissue as she relives his funeral at their little congregational Church of Zion and Phillip's revelation to her at his Enid office. The story further advances to following Ludlow to the Petroleum Building and the files containing the specifications for Charles' evaporative system which were missing from Charles' computer.

"So after locating Ludlow on the building's directory, I felt I'd no recourse but to figure a way to gain entry. After checking, I obtained a job with the cleaning crew, which needed someone for the floors where Ludlow had his office. Then, that Rosie Redmond started spouting she had seniority, and even after they told her it didn't make any difference, as all floors paid the same, she still wouldn't concede. Now, I'm in the building, but the only office I need is out of reach."

"I think they are ready to close. Do you want to see if a bar is open or we can head back to your place?"

"No difference to me. You decide, JJ."

A short walk and he finds a club in the direction of her apartment. Before long, they are locked in each other's embrace on the postage-stamp dance floor.

The feel of her hand in his and the warmth of his arm to her back is only intensified when she feels his warm breath on her neck and as he rises to her ear, he whispers, "You smell very nice--very nice, indeed."

He leaves her at her apartment, but every meeting thereafter, she becomes aware that her heart rate increases at the 'rap tap tap' of his knuckles upon her door.

Is she having feelings for JJ, or is she desperately trying to recapture lost feelings, security, and the safety she felt with Charles-all of which were too quickly snatched from her all those months ago? No, she must explore this!

From then on, Connie knows they would be together every opportunity possible, and each time they would be growing closer. She dreads the thought of not having a reason, any reason, to continue seeing JJ because she finds him captivating in his straightforward and unpretentious ways. Is that her life, being pretentious in her crystal chandelier world? Then the 'rap tap tap' comes, and she smiles as she rises to welcome him. *"Please Lord, don't let me be shattered at the hands of a man, once again!"*

"Hello, come in. Could I offer you something?" Connie states as she releases her on-again, off-again defenses towards her circumstances and life.

He looks her way, and a smile immediately comes to his face. It begins in his velvet brown eyes and continues to his mouth, with those full lips, which look so so soft, and when they had been together before, the urge to lift her hands and touch them has been suppressed-suppressed against caring for someone once more. Now, would tonight be the night she could act on the urge she so desperately wants to act upon, and the many other urges she knew would follow, or would her better judgment contain them?

CONSTANCE SINCLAIR

"All our planning and then we were unable to get the files from Ludlow. And that poor girl, what, oh what was she doing in his office? So many months and another unexpected death."

"I know."

"JJ, you have been such a good friend all these months."

"Come here, Connie. It'll be all right."

As the tears flow, I lean into JJ's embrace as I'd often leaned into Charles' arms for comfort and security. Could that feeling of extreme love be found in the warmth of another man's arms? I had often cried myself to sleep, trying to find some moment in time with Charles in which to recapture that love. Then just as quickly as it came to the forefront of my memories, my emotions would plummet from the highest degree of love one could obtain to the very depths of scorn and disbelief of the situation in which Charles had left me.

Now, here with JJ, and as my thoughts whirled, suddenly our lips met and as we kissed, my emotions ran rampant. I felt the heat rise to my neck while my whole body pulsed, as every nerve was raw and aching. Then suddenly, without warning, JJ rose and left without a further word.

ROSIE REDMOND

"Connie, can we talk?"

"I guess, but this has been a rough couple of days. If this is concerning the police wanting to speak with us about that poor girl once more, I already know."

"No, I hadn't heard that," Rosie answers as she glances away because she is aware of the scheduled meeting. She's the one that got Detective Dobbins' attention after she had forwarded Connie's text to him. "Maybe I'll just wait and go over all this with Detective Dobbins."

"No, come on, you can't start something and not finish it. You know the rule. Besides, girls stick together, so what's up?"

"I have been rolling this around in my head and didn't know whether to speak with you or not."

"Come on, spill the beans."

"Well, there are several things. First, I've been cleaning these grease spots, which have appeared only on the eighteenth and nineteenth floors. I talked to maintenance, as I was certain it was made by moving large equipment or one of the mobile equipment transports, but they said nothing has been moved and then asked me if I had noticed any equipment missing, which I haven't.

Secondly, I found a note on the eighteenth floor's stairwell door, and when I opened the stairwell door to look around for anyone, I found several more spots, or I should say spots, and a grease drag mark as if something had been pulled across each stair.

Connie says, "I haven't seen any spots."

I know," Rosie continues while shaking her head, "This is all very strange and makes my mind hurt."

"Then, thirdly, the night of that poor girl's death, I was mad as I thought Mr. Ludlow had locked his door before I could get in to clean, but I was wrong, as the door partially opened as if something was obstructing my entry. I pulled the door towards me, and as I tried again, it gave way, and that's when I saw that horrible scene and ran to call 911.

And the part I have really been rolling around in my head concerns you, and I'm still not certain if I should bring it up with you or wait on Detective Dobbins to be present?"

Rosie knows she's on a fishing trip for information from Connie as she wants to be able to go back to Detective Dobbins with more information on the text from Connie she forwarded to him a few days before."

"No, please, tell me and give me a chance to see if I might be able to remove your doubts."

Rosie after a deep breath, "I don't know, I keep turning it over in my head."

"I'll make you a deal, if I can't explain the matter to your satisfaction, I'll call Detective Dobbins myself," Connie counters.

Rosie, after a few seconds' pause. "Okay explain this. That night before I ever entered Mr. Ludlow's office, you texted me our distress signal."

"Yes, I remember I did, as I thought I'd heard the stairwell door, and it made my heart race, so I immediately hit 'send' on my phone. There, see that was simple."

"Well, that part was simple, but how could you..." as Rosie hands Connie her phone open to that night's messages..."In exactly one minute, respond back that you were mistaken? Answer me that!"

Connie fidgets, looks off in the distance as Rosie says, "Just as I thought. Something was going on that night, and you know more than you're saying---more about that poor girl's murder."

Now standing and looking down at her, Rosie continues. "You made the deal, sweetie. Start dialing, Missy, or should I make the call to the police for you?"

Connie suddenly breaks into tears while replying, "Oh Rosie, I'm so scared. I'm afraid I know who murdered her and even worse, I think I'm in love with him. I'm in love with a murderer!"

Now, the tears are flowing, and Rosie can't resist mothering Connie as she puts her arm around her shoulders and gives her an "it's all right hug," which is swaying Connie back and forth in little quick jerks. Rosie is so hoping this would help Connie quickly recover, as she hates tearful situations.

"Connie, get a hold of yourself. What was that last part? You think you're in love with a murderer? You're in love with Louis Ludlow?"

"No, I'm in love with JJ."

"I'm lost here. You're in love with the murderer, and it's not Ludlow? You do know the police aren't looking for anyone but Ludlow. Just back up, and let's start over. Go all the way back to your distress message, and go from there."

"I'm out of tissue. I need a tissue!"

"Here," Rosie again shaking Connie back and forth, "Use this cleaning rag. Now, talk!"

"Okay, that note you found was meant for me, but JJ put it on the wrong floor, so he came to find me. He was supposed to leave me instructions on where to meet him so we could get into Ludlow's office before you got there to clean. I remembered you had told me you only locked the office after you were done. Oh, Rosie, what did the note say? Please tell me!"

"I still have it in my smock pocket." As she was digging around she says, "So this JJ person, what does JJ stand for anyway?"

"Jeremiah Jason."

"Okay, give me more, Jeremiah Jason…what?"

"Oh, Jeremiah Jason, Jeremiah Jason Paige."

"Here's the note, a little worse for wear, but here."

Connie slowly reads, while all the time shaking her head, "Oh my, my worse fear realized. "DON'T COME UP" all in capital letters and even an exclamation point." Tears flow, as she fumbles, looking for Rosie's cleaning rag. "He was there in Ludlow's office, in the office where you found the dead girl that night." Crying and blowing, crying and blowing. "I need another rrrraaaagg," now wailing.

Rosie is furiously digging in the supply cart for another half-way-clean polish rag. "Oh honey, here. How did you get into this mess?" and as the story unfolds, Rosie is quite aware that there possibly won’t be enough rags to handle this night on either of their carts.

JEREMIAH JASON PAIGE

How did I let this happen? I came here to locate Charles after Amanda became frantic when she was told he was in an accident. She had finally decided to speak with Charles and voice her concern over the unexpected visit from Ludlow, and if she was safe. However, the hospital wouldn't tell her anything, as she wasn't a family member. Ha! What a laugh.

I checked into Ludlow after I found out Charles had been flown out of state and died before surgery could be performed. I saw Constance at Ludlow's building, and I should have stopped there, but something in her actions and her disconcerted way made her seem so helpless.

I started following her, and she kept returning to the Petroleum building, but entering through the employee's entrance. I became confused until I made my fake meeting at the lounge where she told me she's working the cleaning shift. "Really, Mrs. Charles Sinclair was working as a scrubwoman?" I just had to know more, and then I made the mistake of going to her apartment.

I guess as these last few months passed, I...I, she was just so helpless! How was I to know that I would fall for her? What have I done? Amanda was so upset over her father. How could I betray Amanda, let alone my own sister, after everything that has happened to them both? How can I explain to Amanda that I'm in love with her father's wife? How this accidental meeting can be changing me, changing my every thought and now my life?

I must get out of here before I'm caught in this murder. I have to pack and leave now. Right now!

DETECTIVE DANIEL DOBBINS

"Pete, Pete, get in here."

"I was just heading this way to talk to you. It seems that hit and run death might have just been bumped to homicide."

"Pete just keep your head wrapped around one case at a time, and until the paperwork gets to my desk, it's not officially our case. Anything from the medical examiner on that Jane Doe at the Petroleum Building? And I want to see that toxicology report."

"Let me check."

Now, adding, after Pete has exited his office. "And, what did you find out on those text messages the cleaning lady forwarded to us?"

Pete sticks his head back in the door. "Yuh? The text message? Let me see if the girls have heard back from her cell company. They had to get the Judge to sign off on it before they could obtain the records."

"Pete, see if you can help them any. That's the only lead we seem to have at this time."

Pete returns in a rushed manner. "Nothing on medical examiners or toxicology report. However, you said there's something fishy with the timing. Well, that isn't the only thing that turned up fishy. The other cleaning woman, Connie Clair? Listen to this! Her phone is paid through Sinclair Oil."

"Well, what do you know? Guess that just moved the follow-up interview with the cleaning crew to the forefront."

ROSIE REDMOND

"Oh, Detective Dobbins, I'm so glad I caught you."

"What is it, Miss Redmond? Our meeting is just in a few minutes. Can it wait until then?"

"No, you see, I confronted Connie last evening over the text messages."

"Why? Why would you do that? I specifically told you I would get back with you upon learning anything, and that's precisely what the meeting is about today."

Rosie takes a few steps back as she never expected this demeanor from the detective as all previous calls or meetings they had, he had seemed most pleasant. "I had several unanswered questions that I'd been churning in my mind so...I'm so sorry. I meant to ask Connie only about the text, but I ended up talking with her over all the others, too."

"I don't remember any 'others,' like what?"

"Well, just some grease stains."

"Okay, what else?"

"You see, as I attempted to enter Mr. Ludlow's office, I was met by resistance as the door stopped, but after a second attempt, I was able to enter."

"That's it?"

"No, one more. The note."

"There's a note!! Miss Redmond, you know of a note and just now feel it pertinent to relay this information to me? What were you thinking?" Now, speaking in a less than pleasurable way, "You call and notify me regarding the text but never think to mention these other oddities that would also be pertinent?"

"I, in no way, meant to conceal anything from you. I just was mulling them over in my head, and I guess they just hadn't got to the spoken part until I confronted Connie last night."

"Well, keep it coming, sweetheart, as the time for mulling is past, way past!"

Rosie stammers, as if deciding where to begin.

"Let me make this as clear to you as possible. This was to be a meeting, and then after your first little confession, I thought more like an interview. But now I'm inclined to believe we need a full-blown interrogation that will be held downtown at Colcord Police Headquarters."

"Pete, call for the bus and load this whole cleaning crew. We're going downtown."

Rosie, in a trembling voice, speaking not to anyone but herself, "What have I done? What will Connie think?"

After hearing this, Detective Dobbins says, "Pete, I just changed my mind."

Rosie now elated with his change of heart. "Oh, thank you, Detective, thank you so much. The meeting room here is fine. Thank you."

"Pete, go ahead and call for the bus for everyone except Miss Redmond and Miss Clair. They can ride in the back of two different squad cars; I don’t want them having any contact. Pete, be sure they are in different interrogation rooms, also."

"Got it, Danny. Will do."

Rosie, feeling a slight chill entering her body and increasing in intensity with every thought of her situation, digs for a tissue only to find the well-used polish cloth from the prior night’s encounter with Connie. Without a second thought, she wipes her eyes and blows her nose as she’s escorted to the elevators.

DETECTIVE DANIEL DOBBINS

"Are we all comfy, Miss Redmond?"

Rosie suspiciously eyes the good detective, trying to comprehend if he's being ironic or sincere. Either way, she, is proceeding with extreme caution.

"I'm good, thank you."

"Well, that's just peachy."

Rosie quickly discerns "ironic" as the answer to her question.

"Let's just get started then. After exiting the elevator, you receive a text from Miss Clair, making you believe she might be in danger?"

"Yes, but only a moment later, she says that she was mistaken."

"And you're telling me that was the only thing you thought suspicious associated with the whole evening?"

"No, there were other things, as I told you at the Petroleum Tower. I thought Mr. Ludlow had locked his door, as it usually is open, so I don't have to fumble for my keys, but I was mistaken, because as I turned the knob it released, and I continued to press against it, but there's some type of obstruction. I pulled the door toward me, and then it released. But upon entering the room, there's nothing that would hinder the door from opening the first try."

"Okay, got that. Then you said something relating to spots."

"Yes, I'd started the evening on the eighteenth floor with a stain, then on the nineteenth floor, I found more, and then as I traced the stains, they led me to the stairwell door where I found the note."

"Oh yes, the note. Let's see. Pete said he put it in here someplace." While opening the file, he maintains eye contact with Rosie. He doesn't waiver or blink, thus making Rosie sit straighter in her chair and then reposition herself.

"You do realize how this whole little 'forgotten three or four things' can make me question your intent in withholding information. You can see that, can't you?"

"Oh please, Detective Dobbins, I guess I just got caught up in trying too hard to be able to come to you with something solid. I just kept turning it over in my mind. Then after I confronted Connie, she said she could explain and I...I."

"You just felt the need to play a little with the evidence. Don't you know there's such a thing as chain of evidence, and if exact protocol isn't followed, it makes the evidence, no matter how pertinent to the case, inadmissible?

What exactly were you able to ascertain, and I hope you see the gravity of the situation, Miss Redmond. I know you said at the Petroleum Tower that you were concerned with what Miss Clair would think, so your opinion concerning Miss Clair has changed? It seemed your tone of voice when you contacted me in reference to the text message was less than affable toward Miss Clair's honesty during that night."

"Well, in a way, but after talking to Connie, Miss Clair, I…well, let's say my opinion has softened to some extent."

"Go on."

"After I showed her my phone, with it opened to the text in question, she became very disturbed…"

"Disturbed, in what way?"

"At first, she just looked off in the distance until I pressed her, and then she asked to see the note I'd mentioned while listing all my concerns."

"Yes, your concerns listed to everyone but the proper authorities to handle them. What next?"

"I showed her the note."

"This note?"

"Yes, and she began to tear up, and then she fell apart."

"What brought on the tearful deluge?"

"She stated that the note was left for her, but he put it on the wrong floor."

"He who?"

"JJ Paige."

"Okay, continue."

"And she had no idea what it said, but after reading it, she said that he must have been in the office that night as he was telling her not to come up to Ludlow's office."

"Which night?"

"The night that poor girl was murdered. And then, the waterworks started." Rosie now glances to her hands and stops short of telling that Connie had stated she was in love with him. In love with the murderer! Rosie feels she has betrayed Connie enough and will show some loyalty after their sisterly heart to heart talk the previous evening.

"Sit tight, Miss Redmond. This is beginning to look like a long afternoon, which more than likely will turn into a long night."

Exiting the interrogation room, he hollers, "Pete run this guy through NCIC and state!"

"That's all you got, Danny? Initials."

"Yup, but go in there to Redmond, and see if she knows a first and middle name, then run him. I'll be in with Clair."

"Danny, the rest of this cleaning group checks out clean, and none of them seem to have any information that will be of use. They are getting a little antsy. What do you think?"

"If you have all their names and addresses, let them go."

"Okay," Pete states.

"Miss Clair, sorry to keep you waiting, but as you know, I felt it necessary to continue our visit at headquarters. It seems Miss Redmond had several pieces of information she…let's see, she was turning over in her head. So, if you would like to take up where she left off, it seems you confided in her that you thought you knew the murderer. I must advise you that if I feel you're not very-and I repeat-very honest and straight forward with me, I'll not think twice about booking you as a material witness in this investigation. Are we clear on this? Miss Clair, would you please look at me, and let me know if you understand me completely!"

"Yes, Sir. Yes, Detective Dobbins. I understand and am ready to answer your questions."

"Okay, let's start with something easy, and see if I can fill this legal pad with pertinent information. First thing is, please state your full name."

"Connie Clair."

"Okay Connie, is there any middle name?"

"Louise."

Before continuing, Detective Dobbins sends Pete a message to check Connie Louise Clair, as Pete hadn't been able to find anything at all on Connie Clair.

"The night in question, you were going to meet JJ Paige in Louis Ludlow's office, and for what reason?"

"We were looking for a file that had been taken without permission by Louis Ludlow."

"What sort of file?"

"A file pertaining to oil exploration and injection wells."

"Oh, this is becoming a little less vague. You work for an oil company?"

"No, Sir."

"Miss Clair, I thought you understood that honesty and openness were the only requirements to stay out of jail."

Connie begins to answer while Detective Dobbins glances at his phone and says, "Hold that thought. Please excuse me."

Stepping out the door, he sees Pete headed his direction.

"What did you find on her?"

"Nothing, but I checked her through Sinclair Oil, and they don't know a Connie Louise Clair, but they do know a Constance Louise Sinclair, the widow of Charles Sinclair, who started the company and was CEO. Guess I can tell the girls to cancel that request to the Judge for the phone records."

"To the contrary, keep that ball rolling."

"Can I release Redmond? She keeps banging on the door, wanting out, or keep her in the interrogation room?"

"No, get everything on paper, have her sign it, and then she can go. I'll be in with Mrs. Sinclair, as there's a lot more to this story than we know."

After being confronted, Connie reluctantly relates all the information on JJ and also the Waste Water Evaporative System. She also discloses her belief that Ludlow is the cause, if not the perpetrator, of Charles' fall that resulted in his death.

Detective Dobbins, after repositioning himself from sitting on the interrogation table, then his chair once more leans in the corner, and now scratching his head, reseats himself in his chair as Connie exhaustively keeps her word to tell the whole truth. Every time he moves forward to interject a point or a question, he only falls back as she seems not even to pause for a breath. Finally, she states, "And that gets us to last night and why I'm here now."

Detective Dobbins exhales and looks at the blank legal pad with Connie Louise Clair being the only entry on the whole sheet. Glancing at the cameras in each corner, he stares into the lens, knowing Pete has captured the extensive interview and has probably gotten a good laugh at his impatience, knowing the detective wasn't well versed in letting someone else run the show, which is exactly what Constance Sinclair has done.

CONSTANCE LOUISE SINCLAIR

Leaving the Police Department, Constance regrets declining the offer of a ride home in a patrol car as the skies are dark and thunder rumbles in the distance. She prays this isn't an omen of dark times ahead.

Now home, exhausted but still too hyper to be seated, she paces the room going over the encounter with Detective Dobbins, thinking something was missing. Something, he certainly wouldn't have forgotten to question her over. Could it be Rosie hadn't related to the detective the whole conversation between them from last evening? That must be it! Rosie hadn't told Detective Dobbins that Connie had confessed to possibly being in love with JJ Paige.

DETECTIVE DANIEL DOBBINS

"Finally getting someplace with this case. We should have conducted a second interview with that cleaning woman, but she was such a basket case, I thought there would be nothing else except possibly more hysteria. She unquestionably was playing quite the little detective."

"Pete, what're your thoughts?"

"Well, boss, several things. Ludlow's office was missing any form of computer. There's no desktop, laptop or even tablet to be found. So, this JJ character either took it and didn't tell the Clair woman…I mean, Mrs. Sinclair…or she was with him, and they took it together, hoping it contained the files she was looking for. In addition, those stains and drag marks lead me to think that possibly the body had been moved to that office from an alternate location; we know that's impossible, as that office was definitely the crime scene. And most puzzling, the resistance Redmond encountered while trying to enter Ludlow's office."

"I know. Let's get started by sending the crime scene unit back, and be specific this time about stains on the eighteenth and nineteenth floors. Also, have them check that door and see if there's a problem, either in the mechanism or possibly in the bottom of the door, that's dragging on the carpet. They're the experts. Tell them to do their job, and I want answers!"

"On it."

"Pete, have them check for an alternate door that could let someone exit another direction besides through the main door to that office!"

JEREMIAH JASON PAIGE

JJ places his luggage in the trunk of his car, checks his pocket for his ticket, leans against the car and rubs his head. I can't just leave like this without some explanation. I have to let her know that I need a little time to work through things. Yes, work through things and my alternate life in California and whether it could survive. I can still let her know I'm not just running out on her, just letting things get settled a little. That's it. Just need a little time to think things through. I shouldn't have gone off and left Amanda like that.

CONSTANCE LOUISE SINCLAIR

Connie jumps while placing her hand over her mouth to stifle the urge to scream as the all too familiar rap tap tap can be heard from the other side of the door. Her mind races back through her thoughts and her previous feelings, which has consumed her every moment since leaving the police department. The thought that JJ has murdered that girl, and even if he hasn't he certainly knows something more. Then, as the thunder increases in intensity and frequency, so do her fears. She can hear the wind fiercely blowing as it tosses trees and limbs around beside her windows leaving ghostly shadows on her floor.

Once more, the rap tap tap that used to send her heart racing, as she could hardly wait to get to the door, now makes her release a small, but still audible, gasp.

"Connie, open the door. I'm sorry I left so unexpectedly the other evening. Please let me in. I know you must be confused. Please let me explain. I need to have you understand."

Connie tries desperately to control her now shallow breath. What to do? She grabs her phone to call 911, as she just can't open her door to a possible criminal.

"Connie, please. I'm leaving town, and I can't go like this." Now lowering his voice as he leans against the door and states, "I think I have feelings for you. No, I know I have feelings for you, and I love you. There, I've said it! I do love you. Please, please let me in."

Her heart softens, and her mind immediately reverts to the evening he just rose and left without a word. Was that it? He loves me but doesn't know how to handle it?

As she slowly unlocks the door, with eyes averted, she backs away; the door slowly opens and eases to a stop.

"Connie, I understand your reluctance to see me after I just left, just walked out on you. Please, can we talk? I just need some time to think this through. Can you understand that?"

"JJ, I don't think you do." Connie looks deep into his eyes and tries to discern which JJ she is with at this moment, but the more she gazes at him, looks once again into those velvet brown eyes, she sees nothing but the man she has come to love so completely and now undeniably, whole-heartedly, body and soul.

"You need to think this through? Is it because you have something you need to tell me, something you've kept from me?"

As JJ's mind escapes to California, he thinks of his sister, now deceased and his sister's daughter. "Well, yes, but you have to trust me, and give me a little time and I'll be back."

"Be back. You're leaving?"

"Only for a little while until I can work through this."

"JJ, can't you trust me? We can work through this without you leaving."

"I can't stay Connie; I can't."

While still holding his hands, Connie becomes full of remorse, "JJ, we don't have forever. Life has taught me that. Whatever street we need to turn down, whatever shadows we need to steer through, whatever life has thrown at us, we can survive as long as we have each other. Oh, JJ," while pulling him beside her on the couch, "Can't you see, we can talk with Detective Dobbins and get this done and over."

"Detective Dobbins, what do the police have to do with us?"

"Rosie showed me the note you left on the stairwell door."

"Yes, and..."

"Well, the poor girl. You said, 'don't come up'!"

"Connie, oh, Connie." JJ now rises, releases her hands, and whispers ever so softly, "I have to go...I have to go."

Connie follows him outside where the thunder and wind have turned into a full-blown storm as sheets of rain and claps of thunder hearken to her former premonition of foreboding.

From the corner of her eye, she sees…no; it can't be…as she screams, "JJ, Jeremiah Jason Paige!"

Upon hearing his full name, JJ's mind returns to one of their first conversations, and her reminder that if she ever proclaimed his full name that it would only be if he were in eminent danger.

As, JJ turns toward her voice; police meet him with guns drawn. The handcuffs are applied, his only words to her are, "Connie, what have you done?"

Crying and running toward him, she's only met with restraint as her cries and tears melt with the rain.

DETECTIVE DANIEL DOBBINS

Dobbins, now seated on a desk in the squad room, says, "Pete, which room you got Paige in?"

"Three."

"What's all that?"

"Medical examiner's cause of death and..." says Pete while being interrupted by Danny.

"Well, cause of death surely is blunt head trauma, correct?"

"Yes."

Danny continues, "And let me guess further, the medical examiner names the murder weapon as desktop. Tell me what the toxicology report showed? Anything there?"

"No, just what we surmised, alcohol and not a great quantity at that."

"Sexual assault?"

"None, zero."

"Then, what's the motive for Paige to kill her?"

Pete counters, "Maybe she had the files."

"I'm going to talk to him and see if he will give us an interview voluntarily. Right now, all we know is that he had a juvenile record which was expunged after five years because he stayed out of trouble."

"Hello, I'm Detective Dobbins. Let me apologize for rudely dragging you in here. However, as you know, you're being detained and questioned in the death we are investigating on the nineteenth floor of the Petroleum Tower. Being more precise, the homicide of a young female, early twenties with dark hair. I was wondering if you would speak with me and see if you will be able to shed some light on that for us, would you?"

"I'll try."

"Great, could you please verify that you have been informed of your right to remain silent and to have an attorney present before any further questioning?"

"Yes, the patrol officer read me my Miranda rights before he placed me in the back of his squad car."

"Does the description of the young lady, found dead on the nineteenth floor, bring anyone to mind? Do you know anyone fitting that description?"

JJ, lowering his head answers, "No, Sir."

"Let's move on to something a little easier, shall we? What is your involvement with Mrs. Sinclair?"

"Just friends."

"Could you be more specific? Have you been friends long, and more specifically, how did you meet?"

"A few months back, I noticed her at the Hill Bar and Grill, and we struck up a conversation."

"Just a little friendly, 'how are you and nice to meet you,' conversation or was it more involved?"

JJ now tells of their conversation and how it became known that Louis Ludlow had files possibly taken on the day of Charles Sinclair's dubious fall. He also states that he and Connie had planned to reclaim these files but stops short of saying it was on the night in question.

"On the night of this girl's death, you and Mrs. Sinclair were to be in Ludlow's office?"

"Well, no, we weren't. We didn't go up."

"So you went alone?"

JJ becomes silent, and a stark stare is all that follows the question.

"Mr. Paige? I'll repeat the question. You went alone to the nineteenth floor and entered Louis Ludlow's office?"

No reply is forthcoming as JJ looks toward the corner of the room where, just earlier in the day, Connie had told Detective Dobbins all of their plans.

"Mr. Paige, I must inform you, that as a material witness, I'm given great liberty on your length of stay."

Still no reply. "Pete, get someone up here to escort Mr. Paige to booking."

"What's the charge?"

"I think we have enough probable cause to book him as a person of interest in a homicide."

As the detective stands at the door to leave and while the booking officer unlocks the cuffs restraining JJ to the interrogation table, Pete says, "I told you if we put a tail on that Sinclair woman, it would lead us to this character, didn't I, boss?"

JEREMIAH JASON PAIGE

Now sitting in the holding cell waiting to be processed, JJ can only think of the last words between himself and Connie. "Connie, what have you done?" But she hadn't done it. No, she hadn't turned him into the police. Then what was it that made him believe that she thought he was the murderer? Well, it makes no difference now, as the Detective has that perception. How is he going to get out of this? Now thinking of poor Amanda. *"Amanda, oh, Amanda!"*

CONSTANCE LOUISE SINCLAIR

"Oh Rosie, what have I done? How did this get so out of hand? Do you think they have arrested JJ in this murder? What should I do? Should I go down there? Get a lawyer? Call, please call, and see if you can find out if he has been arrested. Please...Please!"

"Now honey, I woke up at 5:30 this morning, and I tried to go back to sleep, but my mind was talking to myself. I just can't believe that JJ's involved in this in any way, especially not, heaven forbid for you, the murderer."

"Rosie, he thinks I turned him in. He will never speak with me. I don't know; I don't know."

"Why was he here, anyway?"

"He came to apologize for just abruptly getting up and leaving during our kiss."

"He kissed you? You didn't tell me that."

"Yes, and it was our first kiss when I possibly felt I had feelings for him."

"About that."

"About what?"

"You telling me you thought you were in love with him."

"Yeah."

"When I was in the interrogation room, I was giving my reasoning, as clearly as I had it in my mind, for withholding my surmises from the detective."

"Yes, and…"

"And I was telling him all our conversation the previous night at work. Well…"

"Go on."

"I was just feeling so awful about betraying your confidence, that I guess I got a soft heart toward you."

"Aw, Rosie, you have a soft heart towards me? How sweet."

"There's more."

"Okay, but it has to be good if you got a soft heart all of a sudden, right?"

"I know, right? Well, that's when, I stopped short of telling the detective that you thought you were in love with the murderer."

As Connie completely embraces Rosie with a full on body swaying hug, she says, "I knew it; I just knew it."

Rosie, not wanting any part of this display of friendly enamor, stands swaying with Connie, but her arms are tightly pinned to her side, being uncertain if she would embrace Connie even if she could move.

Rosie, now pushing away, says, "JJ came, and he apologized, and that's when they nabbed him?"

"Well, not exactly. JJ also told me that he thought he felt the same towards me."

"Awe, I'm a softy for this stuff."

Rosie, sniffs, shakes her head and continues, "Then, what terrible timing, that's when they nabbed him? I hope it wasn't that nice Pete feller. You know, we sat and talked awhile after that pushy detective left the interrogation room. He leaned forward, looked directly into my eyes, and said he could tell I'd something going on in there. He has a respect for a good mind, well different from that detective. No respect at all from him."

"No, it was a patrol officer. But it was after JJ told me he needed some time to think things over."

"Well, that's understandable. JJ just needs some time to find himself and recognize that he truly loves you."

"Yes, he told me that also."

"Told you what, that he loves you? Boy, you've kept me way in the dark here."

"That's the good part; the bad part was when he told me he had to leave to think about everything. He was leaving, Rosie, just leaving! That's when my mind went to the dark side, realizing maybe he was a murderer, and if not, he certainly knows something of that night's happenings. I looked deep into his eyes to see which JJ I was with." Connie now becomes emotional, but Rosie, still recovering from Connie's previous embrace, takes two steps backward.

"Okay! Now, now. Uh…honey, just settle down a little. You think he could be involved, and he even told you he was leaving, and you still want to continue with this? You sure he isn't running out on you when things get tough? You for certain you want any part of that?"

Connie tearfully answers as she wipes her eyes with a tissue, "Yes, yes, yes, that's where my heart seems to be. I have to do something. Rosie, please call."

"I don't think they will tell us anything over the phone. You better go down there."

"Okay, do I just go in and ask for JJ at the police station and then wait to be called? Oh my, will they pat me down and…"

Rosie, now looking up to heaven as for divine intervention, answers, “For Pete’s sake, come on, and I’ll go with you!”

OKLAHOMA CITY JAIL

"That was a complete waste of time. That officer wasn't the nicest, either. Telling us to check online for visitation rules and we would have known to call ahead to be allowed to visit."

"Rosie, I think I might have, nicely, convinced him to let JJ know that we were at least trying to visit."

"Yes, you were the nice one!!"

Back at her home, Connie kicks off her shoes, and sighs, "It's useless. I shouldn't have even bothered you. I shouldn't have even called."

"No, no, you called the right person. I'm certainly glad you did. Let's see if there might be a better way to help your feller. What have we got left? Let me roll this around a little more in my head and see what my mind can come up with. What has Detective Dobbins not checked as of yet? Or even better, what was he the maddest about…"

"Think, Rosie, think," Connie urges.

"He was pretty mad when I told him about the note and me talking to you."

"What else?"

"The stains, the stains are a real puzzler. They started at the elevator on eighteen, continued to the stairwell and up the stairs to nineteen. Then there's a bigger stain in front of the nineteenth floor stairwell door that started down the hall toward the elevator. Why would they lead to the elevator again? Hum…or did they?"

Rosie now turns and looks squarely at Connie. Connie, hurriedly walks toward Rosie and asks, "What is it? Tell me."

Rosie, with a smile, asks, "What is just to the left after exiting the elevator?"

Connie exclaims, "Ludlow's office!" That's it! Whatever was being hauled went into Ludlow's office. Rosie, you're so smart."

"I know, right?"

“Did you clean any stains in his office?"

"No, but that doesn't mean he didn't. We are going into work a little early tonight, Missy. I knew if I had a chance to do some thinking, it would lead to something."

DETECTIVE DANIEL DOBBINS

"Danny, I'm running Paige straight through the city and county of his residency in California. Also, booking called to say that Paige had a ticket to LA in his coat pocket, and flight date was today."

"Really. When was the return date?"

"No return. It was one way."

"Seems like a lot of people coming and going to the golden state to just be a coincidence. What are the odds that our Jane Doe is from there? Run her prints through the department of motor vehicles and check for a missing persons report in California while you check Paige. There's 90,000 missing persons in the US at any given moment. This should narrow the search."

"Yup, that's my exact thoughts."

“Then match up Paige's cell number to Sinclair's phone records we obtained. Also, let's expand that and see how buddy-buddy Redmond, Sinclair, and Paige are. We might be overlooking the obvious."

CONSTANCE LOUISE SINCLAIR

"Rosie, did you sign us both in?"

"Yeah, and just in the nick of time."

"Why, what happened?"

Saw Ben, as I clocked us both in, and thought for certain he was headed my way to chew me out when I clocked you in, also."

"Oh no, I should have gone to do it."

"Not really, for strangely, he never mentioned it but did say he was waiting to tell me to stay clear of Ludlow's office. Seems Oklahoma City Crime Lab is doing another sweep of the area first thing in the morning. I said he could have left a note like always, and that he didn't have to wait."

"Quick, check your keys. Did he pull Ludlow's office key like last time."

“I’m sure he did. Ben never overlooks anything.”

Rosie now frantically searches her smock pockets and after retrieving the keys awkwardly fumbles through before taking a deep sigh and answers, "No, it's still on here. Ben, Ben, you’re slacking a little, in your old age."

Connie answers, "Oh, thank you, Lord."

"Connie, start your floors, and I'll come for you when I'm certain Ben has clocked out and left."

"Okay."

Connie, donning her smock, hurriedly grabs her cart and heads out.

Rosie sees Ben clock out and exit the building. She watches as he turns up the street but not directly across to the parking lot. Rosie thinks it’s a little odd but doesn’t give it more thought than that as her mind already has enough rolling around in it.

Now out of sight of the building, Ben gives a nod in the direction of a vehicle discretely parked at the end of the block before he crosses to his vehicle.

In a short time, Rosie is at Connie's side. "What are you doing? You're supposed to be cleaning."

"Cleaning? I'm so worried; I can't even concentrate for wondering what JJ must be going through while he thinks the very worst of me. Let's just get up there. I still can't imagine what you hope to find, as the police have been all over that place, but let's go!"

"Right now," Rosie shaking her head, "I don't know for sure myself what I'm looking for, but I'll know it when I see it. Sometimes you have to be in the moment to put stuff together. That's how my head works, and quit rushing me. Hey, don't push!"

With the key entering the lock, both women wait for the click indicating the release of the bolt, and as Rosie lowers the handle, the door opens without resistance as the automatic light sensor activates the lights in the office.

Rosie quickly jumps back.

"What is it? What? You scared me to death!" Connie exclaims.

Rosie turns in a big circle in front of the door. "Two things just came to me. Number one, I remember the feel of the resistance that night, and I would swear it was a person as I recall the movement as if the door was pressing against someone. It wasn't like a hard, stable object which would have been a more abrupt stop."

"Okay, that's good, but what else?"

"The light didn't turn on."

"So?" Connie not seeing any connection.

"Don't you see, the light is a motion light and just now clicked on, because we triggered it by opening the door?"

"So, the girl was in there."

"Yup, but after seeing her that night, I know she wasn't moving any, believe me."

"You don't mean it. You were pushing against the murderer? Oh, Rosie, you could have been killed."

Still standing at the door entrance, with the door only partially opened, and Rosie looking perplexed, Connie slowly says, "Rosie? Rosie, what is rumbling around in your head now?"

"How did the murderer get out?"

"When you ran to call 911! He snuck out then."

"No, I went no further than here," now moving only a few steps to the elevator, "and called from my cell. See, I never took my eyes off that door, as I was trying to absorb what I'd just momentarily saw. And look, the lights are now off from lack of movement."

Upon reentering Ludlow's office, Connie, now close behind Rosie, involuntarily jumps as the lights now illuminate the office, and gives her a brief chill which progresses straight up her backbone to the nape of her neck, making her hair stand on end.

Directly in front of the door is the desk with two file cabinets to the side and the rest running down the back wall.

Rosie drops to one knee as she runs her hand across the carpet, now pristine after the clean-up.

Connie says, "It's been all cleaned. What can we hope to find as there aren't any stains to be found now?"

"Maybe not, but maybe so. You pull a large object up the stairwell, you would surely be out of breath and would have stopped, more than likely right here."

Rosie turns slowly in a circle with Connie, now bending slightly, but staying just one-step behind Rosie as she tries to see what Rosie is seeing, or more than likely what Rosie is rolling around in her brain.

Now walking directly past the desk and file cabinets, Rosie makes a left into the restroom, and as she quickly checks behind the door, Connie is forced to retreat or be hit abruptly in the head.

"Nothing odd in there."

Connie once more falls in step behind the now quickly advancing Rosie. "The closet. It has to be!"

"What has to be?"

"The place the murderer hid to evade detection. He was here the whole time, but we just have to find where."

"You clean this office all the time."

"No, only these last few months as Alice had the upper floors before she retired and I had the floors you currently have."

"But you still have cleaned this office for months and should know every nook and cranny by now."

"I do, but I have to admit, that even I take short cuts. Let me show you something," as Rosie opens the closet which is approximately three feet deep and nine feet long and stepping inside, Rosie, while still maintaining eye contact with Connie, extends both hands and points to each end of the closet.

Rosie with a big smile now exits and is replaced by Connie who gasps and exclaims, "My word, what is all this?"

"My thoughts exactly every time I cleaned and had to maneuver around it."

Connie still taking it all in, says, "Look at all this stuff. Some of it looks nasty, and others are caked with red mud, and I know exactly where that red mud, more than likely, came from."

"Let's hope I have some gloves in my smock, because this whole mess is going to get moved."

Now, Rosie and Connie look at the pile of clothes, boots, coats, a set of mud encrusted waders and even an inflatable dingy, haphazardly stuffed back in its container, all lying in the middle of the office floor.

Each, looks at the other, as both try to catch their breath. Now, without a word, they simultaneously turn to enter the closet with childlike scavenger-hunt mentality.

Connie goes to the right, as Rosie turns left. They both drop to their knees, feeling the base of the walls at each end of the closet.

Connie is the first to speak. "This carpet is tight against the bottom of the wall, and I don't…"

Rosie interrupts abruptly. "Mine's not. I can feel air movement."

While never rising to regain her footing, Connie, in a flash, is directly behind Rosie. "Let me feel. Yes, it's completely different from the other end I was checking. What do we do now? Call Detective Dobbins?"

Rosie now incensed, "Are you nuts? I have come this far, and I'm figuring the rest of this out. Why didn't we bring some tools?"

"Don't you mean a stick of dynamite? That end of the closet feels quite sturdy to me."

"There has to be some way to gain entrance."

"Oh Rosie, don't you remember how upset the detective was? He used some pretty convincing words during my interview."

"Well, isn't that just ducky. You had an interview. Let's see, mine could be described as an interrogation, and the wording was a little past 'pretty convincing' to more in line with sarcastic and downright rude. I'm gonna one-up his book-learned investigative skills and even show up his crime lab people."

Rosie, red-faced and downright agitated, not to mention the fierce madness for which this auburn-haired woman is so well known, now lets out a vengeful scream while simultaneously kicking the panel with all her might.

Connie makes a timely withdrawal as Rosie is propelled backward and lands in Connie's former spot.

Rosie rights herself off her backside to her knees and continually glances from the end of the closet to Connie and back to the end of the closet.

Connie scampers trying to pass Rosie, as her curiosity has gotten the best of her, but Rosie grabs Connie's smock and pulls her to the side, just enough, to let Rosie crawl past her.

"I didn't do all this not to enter first," exclaims Rosie.

"Well, hurry it up," Connie replies.

As they both, wide-eyed, enter the small enclosure, they just as quickly exit. Connie has both hands over her mouth, and Rosie is still wide-eyed.

Connie is first to speak as Rosie paces the floor in front of the desk. "What do you think it is?"

"To my thinking, nothing is ever good when it's concealed in a locked barricaded room and shrouded in black plastic!"

Rosie now walks, with determination, back toward the shrouded items' location but is intercepted as Connie grabs Rosie's arm and with all her force, in an effort to halt her, ends up pulling them both to the floor.

"What are you going to do? Please, for both our sakes, we cannot open that…that…that possible dead body. I'm calling Detective Dobbins."

Rosie, now sprawled on the floor with Connie on her knees to Rosie's side, finally nods assent. Rosie's surrender is to no avail, as they glance to the doorway and see someone they are not expecting.

"Well, hello, ladies," Detective Dobbins says with a big cat-in-the-hat, smile."

DETECTIVE DANIEL DOBBINS

"It's our pleasure to have you two ladies for a return visit, and I appreciate it so much your compliance with my request to not speak to each other during our drive down to headquarters, for, believe me, I could summon another squad car."

"Mrs. Sinclair and Miss Redmond, let's get comfortable in Room 3, shall we?"

"Certainly, Rosie answers, in a sweet as honey voice, as she simultaneously gives a nonchalant head jerk towards the detective and then comes to an immediate halt, abruptly dislodging Pete's grasp on her elbow."

"Mrs. Sinclair? He called her Mrs. Sinclair and not Miss Clair!" Pete now looking to move Rosie into the interrogation room, where he could feel secure and didn't have to fear any retaliation on her part, says, "Let's go in here and get comfortable, shall we?"

Rosie now knows the jig's up. She silently sits as she chews this over in her mind.

Detective Dobbins states, "You see I possibly thought you, Miss Redmond, were being a little deceptive, but now I see it was Mrs. Sinclair as well."

Connie straightens in her chair, and as she starts to defend herself, Detective Dobbins raises his hand and signals her to silence.

"Our little enticement, with the help of your supervisor, Ben, just strengthened my suspicions. As I was going to say, I appreciate you clearing that up for me. We already had a good idea that you two were working together after we received the judges signed summons to seize your phone records. These records revealed the number of phone calls you two exchanged and especially at key moments. For example, your call immediately after important events in this case and most recently the arrest of JJ after he left Mrs. Sinclair's apartment seems to add credence to our suspicions. You see, Mrs. Sinclair, it took you less than 5 minutes to phone Miss Redmond. "

"But…"

Sorry, no buts, please. You're to listen, and I'll do the talking."

Now standing and walking to the mirrored window, he continues his one-way conversation, as Detective Dobbins is no longer going to give Mrs. Sinclair the opportunity to take control, as he was well aware during their previous interview, she certainly had a way of dominating the interrogations. "I thought it most interesting, after leaving your residence, Mr. Paige was quoted as saying, 'Connie, what have you done?' Then during our interrogation of Mr. Paige, he abruptly ceased speaking when I ask if he and you, Mrs. Sinclair, entered Ludlow's office on the night in question. I began to think there might be something he was hiding or someone he was protecting.

Forensics has told us that there's a void spot in the blood spray pattern, in the shape of a computer indicating that the assailant left with the computer. Forensics also told us that Mr. Paige's fingerprints were on the entrance door coming and going on eighteen and the entrance door coming and going on nineteen. But to my surprise, the report also states that prints on Ludlow's office entry door handle were that of Miss Redmond, but expectantly, the prints on the opposite side, being the exit handle the murderer would have had to use to leave, are still unidentified. Still further, and you might find most interesting, there's no transfer blood in any of the prints left by Mr. Paige."

Connie cannot contain herself at this revelation and exclaims, "Oh, that's wonderful."

"You would think so, and I guess it is for Mr. Paige, as he has been released from custody and cleared, even though he was only being detained as a person of interest in this homicide. But as that clears Mr. Paige, even though he didn't feel like sharing what he knew, that brings us to you two."

Now circling their chairs, as coming in for the kill, Detective Dobbins announces, Pete, call booking and send them down."

Both women gasp. Connie's head drops as Rosie falls back in her chair and Pete asks, "What's the charge, person of interest?"

"I believe not. Let's move this up a notch to material witness in a homicide. We could quite easily preface that with hostile, also."

OKLAHOMA CITY POLICE DEPARTMENT BOOKING

"This is a fine pickle we find ourselves in. Come down here to get your feller out, and look who's in!" exclaims Rosie with arms crossed and chin tucked close to her chest.

Connie, as she stares at the small barred window, states in a melancholy voice, "But, oh Rosie, JJ has been cleared. Do you realize what that means? It means we're free to pursue our lives together."

Rosie, now chuckling and circling the holding cell, burst into unabated wild laughter, "Yes, you can say that again, you're completely free. Free as a bird, and that's what you need to be to get out of here, a bird! Snap out of it. JJ may be out, but now we're in!"

"JJ will come for us. I know he will."

"You put a lot of faith in people don't you," Rosie sarcastically states. "You haven't been in the real world much, have you?"

"Charles always said I was naïve, but I guess you're closer to correct than I would like to admit. I have always belonged to somebody. I don't think that's anywhere close to wrong. I was always a daddy's girl, and if I wanted anything, I just got it, and Daddy paid. Then, I met Charles, and I was still very young when we fell in love. We had a short engagement before we were married."

Connie, now rising, walks toward Rosie. "I left one morning, very happily, to return only a few short hours later to a horrific scene. That scene soon turned into a nightmare that left me wasted. During this nightmare and the short time before Charles' death, I attempted numerous times, to just once more see into the eyes of my husband, see into the eyes of the only man I'd ever known."

Oh, Rosie, loneliness is like being homesick all the time. My Mother always said, there's no sickness worse than homesickness. You hurt so much; you want to run back to your secure spot to the one you love so deeply, but no matter how hard and far you run, your love is always just beyond reach."

"I'm so sorry, sweetheart."

"And I appreciate that so much, Rosie. It just seemed after Charles died, I was in a different season of my life than others in my circle of friends. However, I know I was blessed to be in his life and to be so deeply loved by him. Being loved by someone you're so in love with, is a perfect relationship. You know, it's like being where the sun is shining on you all the time."

Rosie with a heavy sigh, "No, I don't know. I have never known that kind of love. Oh, there have been fellers now and then, but I have never been to where you have. Your love must have been incredible, and now, love might have come your way a second time. Connie, Connie, Connie, how fair is that?"

"Rosie, I didn't mean to upset you. I'm so sorry. You see, that's another thing I've never been good at and am trying to change."

"What's that, upsetting people? Because I think you're quite good at that!"

Connie, showing a broad smile, says, "No, silly, saying I'm sorry. There are people that just misuse the word to the point of being meaningless, and then, there are people like me that never let it escape their lips. But don't get me wrong, I always ask the Lord to help bridle my tongue. Charles and I had a pact, from the time of our first disagreement: 'never say anything in the heat of the moment that a thousand apologies can never erase.' You can ask for forgiveness from a person, and they can tell you you're forgiven, but there's no way their subconscious mind could let go of it because you hurt them so deeply that it will be with them always. Just have faith, Rosie, and be open to every opportunity that God puts before you because it's not God's will that we live this short life alone. Everyone deserves to have someone with whom to grow old, and that will be true for you, I'm certain of it."

Rosie starts to interject, "I don't know, Connie. But I so hope it's true and…."

Then suddenly, they are startled back to their current situation, as the sound of the electronic lock mechanism in the cell door jars it open and they hear, "Okay ladies, follow me."

Both now in unison ask, "Where to?"

"Back to interrogation."

DETECTIVE DANIEL DOBBINS

"Boss, what are you up to? You know they were cleared, right along with Paige, as their prints weren't on the office's exit handle."

"I know, Pete, but just wanted to give Paige a chance to jump-ship and possibly head to California. California Department of Motor Vehicles has given us verification that Cassie Walters is our Jane Doe. Paige will be under surveillance if he heads to California, and if he stays, well, we will be watching. Also, wanted to let the ladies stew a little."

"Pete, you talk with them this time, and see what Redmond has to add to this picture, especially regarding her conduct today in Ludlow's office."

"Okay, then back to holding or booking them in?"

"No, release!"

PETE

"Miss Redmond, Mrs. Sinclair, sorry for this little detour you had to take today."

Rosie, now perky, "Oh, I'm sure it's no fault of yours, as you seem always to be most cordial."

Connie turns in her chair, behind the stainless topped table, to get a better look at her usually "less than pleasant" friend. *What is going on here?*

Rosie continues in her perky manner and tells her full summation of what had been concluded in Ludlow's office earlier. As Connie listens, she's amazed at the number of ways Rosie explains her thoughts that she always prefaces with something about 'my mind talked with myself.' *"How many people are in there??"*

JEREMIAH JASON PAIGE

What happens when she finds out, that from the start, I was using her?

CONSTANCE LOUISE SINCLAIR

"Rosie, I just had to talk with someone. He's gone!"

BREAKING NEWS

Oklahoma City, Oklahoma (News9) A break in the case of an unidentified female found in Petroleum Tower Plaza. France authorities report they have in custody a person of interest on an unrelated charge.

THE LAW OFFICES OF DRISCOLL AND DRISCOLL FOUNDERS TOWER OKLAHOMA CITY, OKLAHOMA

Connie, after parking, walks toward the large circular building, as memories of dining at the revolving restaurant on the top floor, flood her way. It hadn't been that long ago, but it seemed an eternity. She could remember what she, as well as Charles, was wearing and remember the feel of belonging to someone when exiting the elevator; she knew a familiar hand would be on her back guiding her. A familiar voice would tell the hostess, "Yes, a table for two," and then his arm would be around her waist, once more taking charge. But not today, no valet parking, and no one to open the door upon entering the building. Yes, Connie, this is truly a different season, a season to which you must become accustomed.

Connie sees Phillip Chapman waiting in the lobby and says, "Phillip, thanks so much for making the trip from Enid to be here and taking over during my absence. I appreciate it so much. I hope I'm not imposing, as you are the only one I could think of to call. I know I keep turning to you as you were the first person I called after Charles passed. And since you informed me of our, or I should say, my financial situation, well, I once more, asked you to step in and continue the quest of solving this problem while I was away. I now, though, have the time to delve into this and see exactly where I stand. You do think the firm has been able to come to some consensus on determining the source of the estate's money shortage?"

"Yes, Connie, that's what I've been advised, and by the time we leave today, it should be crystal clear what has occurred."

"Mr. Chapman, Mrs. Sinclair, please follow me to the conference room."

Now walking the outer circle of glass windows, the numerous balconies, on any other occasion, would be tempting to step out, sit and drink in the panoramic view. How remarkable and awe inspiring. *Could I ever hope for a time, any time, where that thought would be pure instinct instead of conceptual?*

As the conference room door opens, Connie notices the large crystal lighting; the only wood in the room is the elongated oval table with high back leather chairs. The entire front wall is glass, thus placed, to leave the view unobstructed.

"Phillip, do come in."

"Hello, Arthur."

"Connie, this is Arthur Driscoll. Arthur, may I introduce Mrs. Constance Sinclair?"

"My pleasure entirely, Mrs. Sinclair. Please be seated."

"May I further introduce my partner and brother, Matthew, and our Investigator, Deidra Hulbert?"

"Phillip, I'm sure, has informed you that immediately at the conclusion of our meeting, we have asked your accounting firm to meet with you. We felt that both matters were intertwined and should be addressed in the same manner, jointly."

"I hope that's to your liking, as well."

Connie, only nods, confirming both details have been conveyed. As she listens to the first Mr. Driscoll, she is encouraged to feel that old familiar sense of pride for her husband. That pride that she so often felt, as Charles, never boastful, just always a forward thinker, continued with his idea to minimize or maybe completely negate the need for the use of injection wells in the oil fields.

Phillip, interjects his theory that the evaporative system can still be brought to fruition upon the discovery, or as Connie is certain the word should be recovery, of the prototype plans.

Now, a distant sound comes to her along with chills.

As the meeting continues, and as the final piece of information is being relayed to the group by Investigator Deidra Hulbert, Connie hears the undeniable sound of thunder, which chills her to the bone. Then as the investigator says, "a sizeable estate in California has been located." More thunder accompanied by her ever present feeling of foreboding once again manifests itself.

While the room fills with the accountants, who can only be described as narrow-eyed, balding and stoop-shouldered, the storm outside intensifies. Phillip looks Connie's way and asks, "Connie, are you all right? You're completely ashen. Would you prefer we stop and continue this at another time?"

Suddenly, Connie is intensely aware that every eye in the room is looking her direction, she then closes hers as she thinks, *"Oh Lord, what are they going to tell me that could have me in such a state? Lord, I need you. Please get me through this."* Taking a relieved but also, peaceful breath, she opens her eyes as she has given everything to the only One she knows who gives peace and controls the earthly rage of the storm outside.

She listens to numerous accountants while flipping through another organized, tabulated, and collated and whatever other "lated" word of which you can think, as the final dagger to her heart, the words Bordillon Estate, Northern Los Angeles County, is mentioned. So there's her answer. The largest part of the monies has been used in conjunction with this estate. It's the consensus of all concerned in this joint meeting of attorneys, accountants and, yes, even Phillip, that Connie might be able to retain the house and land by liquidating all the non-structural assets associated with her home.

Connie takes a deep breath then forces the words, “Thank you all for your endeavors, and Miss Hulbert, may I speak with you?”

“Certainly, Mrs. Sinclair,” Miss Hulbert says while taking the seat next to Connie. “How may I help?”

“First, thank you for your information on the California estate.”

“You’re welcome.”

Connie continues, “You’re confident money has been sent to California?”

“Yes, the bulk of your money has been going to secure the stability of the Bordillon Family.”

“Bordillon? Isn’t that of French ancestry?

“Yes, there’s a town in France by that name, Bordillon.”

As Connie pushes away from the once massive oval conference table, which at this moment, seems dwarfed in comparison, as it’s now filled to capacity with the vast number of personnel these two firms employ, she knows one thing for certain. She is just praying that the asset liquidation will possibly cover their sizable fees, which will certainly be on the top of the pile of other bills.

As she looks at the two large binders, containing her total worth, she's praying to be released from this moment, this office, without having to express anything more than complete thanks and gratitude.

Phillip offers to have the large binders and other documentation delivered to Connie later in the day as she thanks him for attending. She smiles and nods to the others, which is her all too common way of covering her emotions, other people's derogatory comments, or other's lack of tact.

Exiting the building, she sees that the storm has passed and all that's left is distant rumbles and Connie, for a second time, thanks the Lord for taking care of her, once more.

DETECTIVE DANIEL DOBBINS

"A break in the case and this time, in our favor. The prints received from the French authorities, where Louis Ludlow is in custody, are a match to the inside door handle prints that also contained trace blood from the victim. This should be enough to obtain a warrant for extradition from France. Please tell me we have an extradition treaty with France?"

"We certainly do."

"It seems the implement company caught Ludlow on embezzlement when he missed a quarterly payment. There's an interest default clause that his former assistant, Cassie Walters, always handled and of which Ludlow wasn't aware."

FRENCH PRISON CELL
SAVEUR, FRANCE
LOUIS LUDLOW

"Embezzlement? I can't be charged with embezzlement. You have no proof! Just check, there's no payment in default by close of business, June 30."

"Maybe that's correct, Monsieur, but when we were contacted by your employer, while you were on a leave of absence, they found the account in question, when it was flagged through an interest default clause that a Miss Walters always handled. The account may have been repaid that's in question, but you forgot the interest default clause that was activated when no payment was made in the third quarter and your name came to the forefront when you made the double payment in the fourth quarter. Why I'm visiting with you, also, is to inform you we have now been notified that you're wanted in the United States for the murder of Miss Walters. Was this the reason?"

"No, indeed. I know nothing of any such clause, much less the need to attack a woman over mere interest. I have money coming shortly. I have a piece of equipment I want my company to manufacture and market in the United States. I didn't know and was never aware of Miss Walters being in Oklahoma, as she had left the company's employment to work for one of our competitors. Anyway, I wasn't privy to any of this, as Cassie handled all that. As I told you, the only reason I came to France in the first place was to try to get a patent, which would be equivalent to a United States patent, for the evaporative system to replace the injection wells so it can be marketed in the United States. This could be very lucrative for my company. I need to speak with the director at my company as he will certainly concur."

"I'll leave you now, Monsieur. Please let me know your decision on an Avocat to represent you." Now exiting, "Also the United States is filing extradition proceedings for your return to stand trial on the charge of Murder."

Alone and his head now in his hands, Louis, silently addresses his former co-worker. *"Oh Cassie, Cassie, why did you have to do that to me?"*

Louis Ludlow has no idea the noose is slowly closing, and ironically, being closed by Cassie.

Now remembering that fateful night in his office at the Petroleum Tower with…

CASSIE WALTERS

"I must say, your office has a striking view, and Louis, it's wonderful of you to take me out for dinner and show me Oklahoma City."

As she turns, she notices he isn't focused on their conversation as he's ogling her contours. She continues trying to get him back to the moment as she asks, "This chair, is it real leather?"

"Oh huh. I'm not sure if it is or not. Yes, sure, I guess."

She continues, "The Murrah Bombing Memorial was a complete and entirely new experience for me. How solemn. I felt as if I'd left a funeral after we walked the area. What a senseless act of cowardice. But in contrast, Bricktown is such a novelty and that all was abandoned warehouses. Amazing!"

Chattering on, she continues in her attempt to open up the conversation. "The dinner at the Mantle, well, I don't believe I have been so well fed in my whole life."

"My pleasure! I'm glad I could show you the downtown area. You know, I have you staying at the Skirvin, which is very prestigious. There's a lot of history there."

"Oh, well, we must walk through it before I leave."

"I have been told the piano bar, where, I believe, the piano is a stunning red color, is well worth a stop."

As his mind regresses to their meal, Louis recalls, "I had to chuckle when the waiter stammered between, and what would Mrs. or I mean your daughter, no, your companion tonight be ordering? He was so red faced that when the check came, I left him a $100 tip with a happy face drawn on it. I considered it a compliment that he even entertained the idea that we were a couple. What do you think, Cassie? Do you think it unconceivable that someone would consider us a couple?"

She glances his way and ponders her options. "I guess, I never have thought much about it." Cutting her eyes away from his, she tries once more to change the subject. "I had no idea this plant is real. What exactly is it?"

With no answer to her question, he continues down the same road. "I know when we worked together, you had to have noticed my eyes going wayward at different times."

"No, sorry, I guess not." Cassie quickly says as she decides just to get down to the real reason for this trip and get out of here.

"Louis, have you done anything more with those files I got converted for you?"

Cassie, you never saw that I sent looks your way?"

Now from the back moving closer and touching her left arm with his left hand and lower right back with his other, he attempts to turn her into himself.

"Louis, I'm trying to speak to you about the files I converted." Now facing him and seeing the look of lust in his eyes, she backs ever so slightly and while trying to stay composed, she continues, "After I studied my copy, it looks like oil well conversion equipment. An oil site waste water evaporation system, to be more precise."

Louis suddenly bristles as any further sign of lust had now been replaced with vile contempt. "What did you say?" Drawing his words slowly out, while advancing.

"I'm speaking of the oil site specs, Louis."

"No, before that, before that you said, ‘you studied your copy’," now spitting the words through clenched teeth. "So that's why you called with your sweet little 'dripping with honey' words, ‘I'm going to be in Oklahoma City and would love to spend some time with you.’ You think you’re going to romance me into telling you something, you’re out of your mind."

"No, Louis, not at all, nothing like that," Cassie states as her voice rises, while she struggles to see what is behind her and if there’s any place that might reveal a point of escape.

Louis quickly advancing, says. “Where are you going? I'll show you what snooping into my business gets you."

As he moves forward, she continues her retreat, but to no avail, as he deftly smashes her head repeatedly against the glass covering of his desk which shatters with the final forceful blow.

PHILLIP CHAPMAN

"Connie, I'm calling on the sale. I don't think it wise for you to be present. Please consider Joyce and me attending in your place."

"Phillip, thank you. That's so kind of you. I just received the Sale Bill from Reading Auctioneers; it shows three days for the sale, and the brochure is very thick. Could that be possible?"

"Yes, I'm afraid so. There's a lot to sell, and the auctioneer wants a key piece of asset on each day to keep the buyers interested and returning. The items in the residence will be auctioned in the house, so you don't want to be in residence then."

"I haven't been to the estate but a few times since that day I left your office. You remember you called soon after."

"Yes, I remember. Connie, we can't act as your proxy, but we will be glad to attend as an advocate and contact you for any information or details that might have been overlooked. Connie, are you there? Connie? Hello, Connie?"

Answering, but in a disturbed voice and now cracking a little, "Phillip, the centerfold."

"Hold on. Let me turn to it. Oh Connie, I know, I'm so sorry."

"Phillip, I feel Charles' presence right now. He understands and is trying to comfort me."

"That's wonderful, Connie. I know it must have been a little unnerving for you upon turning to that picture."

"They have him so prominent, as well he deserves. It was just a shock, but he deserves the entire centerfold to show all his beauty. My beautiful boy, my beautiful Black Magic."

"You okay?"

"I'm not certain, Phillip. I'm trying to think of Magic in someone else's care. It's like giving a child to another to care for. This can't be. There must be some way I can retain Magic through all this. Phillip, I'm not at all certain I can do this! You are checking the value of my jewelry, aren't you? I have some high-quality jewels, which should bring enough for me to retain Magic."

"Connie, take a minute, and please be seated as I want you to be able to think clearly. Can you do that for me?"

"I don't know. Maybe we could continue this conversation later."

"No, Connie. Please take your time but do not hang up the phone, please! We need to visit more on your jewelry."

It seems like an extraordinary amount of time to Phillip as he hears the heart-wrenching cries of someone who has lost her first love and now is realizing the emotions revisited through her husband's death and the probable loss of another love. Her beloved Magic.

Phillip leans back in his chair and unashamedly catches the slow but increasing tears running from his eyes. He releases his grief for the loss of his friend and for the pain being suffered by his friend's wife, who now is physically and emotionally distressed to her very being, and he's, momentarily, going to release more upon her. *"How much can one person handle? Lord, sustain her as only you can."*

"Connie?" but no answer as he hears her guttural sobs subside to some extent. "Connie!"

"Phillip, Phillip, I miss him so much. I miss who we were. I miss the security of knowing everything would be all right as long as we had each other. But most of all, Phillip, most of all, I miss his touch and the ever present kiss to my forehead that would invariably be followed by his all-engulfing hug and more kisses. How can I possibly live without him and now Magic? How can I go on not knowing how Magic will be cared for? There has to be some way for me not to have to bear the loss of Magic. Has to be!"

"Connie, you're right. We should speak later. Please know Joyce and I love you. Get some rest, and we will talk later."

Phillip says to himself aloud, after placing the receiver in its cradle, "Yes, we will talk later, talk later. Bye, Connie. But I have to do something.

I just can't tell her." At that moment, Phillip also feels Charles' presence.

Connie, now stumbling to her feet, "Let me get to the door. My cellular coverage is terrible in here. I only have two bars. Okay, Rosie, can you hear me better? Good, now start over."

"Do you have a cold? You sound all congested?"

"No, I was just on the phone with a friend and trying to grasp the magnitude of the pending sale of assets. Needless to say, it's quite a lot to digest."

"Oh, sure, honey. I can understand that. Must be very traumatic. I can't even wrap my head around it."

"Rosie, you have turned out to be such a great and supportive friend. If I were there, I would give you a hug. You know I love hugs, particularly passed along to friends."

"Yup. Yupper. I remember your embraces," as Rosie vividly recalls one of the most impressive, the full frontal embrace. This hug not only pinned both her arms to her sides, she was certain her cleavage was pushed to a most impressive stance, "but I've got information on Jane Doe."

"Oh, with all that's going on, I'm ashamed to admit, Jane Doe hasn't been at the forefront of my mind."

"Now, honey, that's understandable. You don't think another thing at all concerning that. As you know, I'm the one keeping up with everything, and it's all locked securely in my head. I mull it all over every now and then."

"You don't say. I didn't realize you were back in Detective Dobbins' good graces. My last impression was quite the opposite. I got the impression we were dismissed from his sight, and he, hopefully, thought we weren't to return."

"Yes, sweetie, but I've been holding out on you. Well, not holding out, but more like, just haven't had the opportunity to visit with you any."

"So, what's the big revelation or should I restate that to be, who is the big revelation?"

"I don't know if you happened to notice, but every time we were at police headquarters, Pete just gravitated my way. It seemed, well, you remember, Detective Dobbins always put you in one interrogation room, and Pete always managed to be with me in another room. Well, it was during one of these times when he was trying to find out how my head worked, and I told him I was rolling things around in my mind. You know how I do that?"

"Un huh, I know that's a prominent trait of yours."

"Well, it seems Pete had observed that…uh…trait in me, also. He said, 'Rosie, I have noticed that when it comes to you.' All the time, Connie, he was looking deep into my eyes."

"During another interrogation, he said, 'I think that's what draws me to you, your mind.' That might not be his exact words, but I know that's what he meant to say."

"Anyway, we have been out a couple of times and we talk quite often on the phone."

“Rosie, how exciting, I’m so happy for you.”

“I know, right?”

“Okay, so back to the case. What did he tell you?”

“Oh, right. Well, guess who is in custody in France?”

“I have no idea. Who?”

“Louis Ludlow from the nineteenth floor, the murder office!”

“Did you say, France?”

“Yup, the French authorities sent his prints, and they have confirmed they are a match to the office door handle. Connie, are you there?”

“Yes.”

“I thought I’d lost you. You know, only two bars.”

"No, I'm here. France? You're certain he said France?"

"Yes. Isn't that wonderful to finally have an end to all this?

Connie?"

"AN END! You would think so, Rosie, wouldn't you?"

CONSTANCE LOUISE SINCLAIR

I suddenly awake…to what? I hear the wind, and then thunder as the rain is pouring.

As I lay, I wonder what the winds of my memory will reveal.

Ludlow in jail in France and the money funneled to the estate in California bearing a French name. Could there be a connection between Louis and Charles?

PHILLIP CHAPMAN

"Connie, this is Phillip. I hope I've caught you well rested from our previous visit."

"Yes, I'm better. Thanks for asking."

"When we spoke last, there's something I wanted to discuss with you. You had asked me to determine the value of your jewels and possibly use them to obtain Magic at the sale."

"Yes, Phillip. The night the portrait of Magic was unveiled, I told Charles to take all my jewels and those in the vault and use them for whatever purpose he chose as that was the first time I'd ever heard of any financial difficulty."

"Connie, there's no easy way to say this. Your jewels were all paste replicas."

"Connie?"

“I’m here, Phillip.” In a soft, subdued voice, “I’m here. I understand completely.”

Phillip astonished at her composure, thinks he needs to repeat this, in his way of thinking, bombshell.

“So, there’s no way to save Magic from the auction?”

Phillip, now shaking his head at this woman‘s pure self-control, replies, “No, but you have to understand, the whole intention of this sale is the hope of being able to retain your home. Even if you were able to retain ownership of Magic, you couldn’t afford the workers to tend to the stables much less pay his trainer, Doug Hartly.”

“Phillip, that’s it. Doug needs to have Magic. He certainly can see the value of Magic. That’s it. Magic will be secure in Doug’s control. I can live with that.”

“That might be a tall order. You have to understand that there’s no guarantee of this happening, but I’ll do what I can.”

"Thanks, Phillip. Please, you and Joyce attend the sale in my place, and tell Joyce I send my love and hugs."

"I will but how…how do you do it? How do you keep going? This should have done you in."

"Oh, Phillip, believe me, I'm not the stalwart you envision. I'm just…just, all cried out. There is no one to lean on now. You see, there has always been someone to care for me. It's time for me to regain control of my life and I just have to give it to God. We are only guaranteed this small moment in time, and we don't always understand the situation, but we do know who is in control."

CONSTANCE LOUISE SINCLAIR

"Rosie, I haven't spoken with you in a while. How are you?"

"I'm good, honey. But I should be asking how you are?"

Connie slowly says, "Okay, I guess."

"Well, that doesn't sound very convincing."

"I'm all settled back in the house."

"That big ole place. What are you doing for furniture? I feel bad, I should have come, and we could have gone to some tag sales to get you a few things. I'm sorry I didn't think of that."

"That's okay. I slept several nights in front of the fireplace as I have all the rooms which are equipped with zoned heat and air turned off until I hang on a couple of months and see where I am financially. Being alone hasn't been as scary as I'd envisioned. The unknown is always frightening and I'm trying to take control of my life by not depending on others, by being my own person.

Phillip and Joyce bought my bed and the two chairs in the alcove and had them placed back in my bedroom. Another friend bought my orchids, and all have been returned to their original location. Also, listen to this, Rosie, this brings me to tears. Jesse, one of our drivers, bought the items from his RV section of the horse hauler which he stayed in when on the road transporting the horses to shows. When he found out I had no kitchen or bath items, he brought them to me one evening. Oh Rosie, I have found friends are truly God's angels.

Tonight, I fixed myself a salad and ate in the garden. I can't remember when this place has ever been this quiet. As I walked among the flowers, I stopped to fill an empty birdbath and looked at the hydrangea. The marker said, 'Sister Teresa' all pure white with a few clusters having a beautiful green edging. You know, green is my favorite color, and 'Sister Teresa' was exactly what I needed to hear. My friend, Jamie, calls that 'God Winks.' I even pulled a few vines of run-away ivy that somehow made its way to the top of the Rose of Sharon. You should come out!"

"I know I should. You're not that far, are you?"

"No, just get on the Kilpatrick North and take Highway 3 West, and then I'm just a few miles. We sit on the north side of the highway, just before Uncle John's Creek."

"You sound remarkably clear. You get a new phone?"

"No, I'm still in the garden on the bench Charles and I always sat on. If this bench could talk, I know it would tell some great stories. Wish I had them all written down.

Rosie, Ludlow is being extradited from France. His company is dropping the embezzlement charges after finding out he's indicted for the murder of one of their former employees. I guess that's good."

"Yes, I knew. Pete told me."

"I can't believe it's been almost two years since Charles left."

Rosie says, "That doesn't seem possible. Are things getting any better?"

"Yes. My circumstances shouldn't be like this for long. Or that's my hope. I have enough money for maintenance on the property and thank you, Lord; the oil wells are picking back up slowly. God is good, Rosie."

"I know He is. The Bible tells us, good comes from all things, and my good has arrived through me meeting Pete."

"I'm so happy for you, Rosie. So happy."

"I wasn't going to bring this up, but I feel like I should tell you something. I need to tell you something about JJ. Do you want to know or not? I don't want to do anything to bring you more heartache, Connie. I don't want to hurt you."

After a long pause, "I don't know. It's been so long. Oh Rosie, I actually don't know."

"Talk with you later, Sweetie. Pete's here."

Connie, now leaning her head back on the all too familiar bench, sees God‘s stars lighting the night, and says, “Star light, Star bright, first star I see tonight. Wish I may, wish I might...Oh Lord, could it be Charles, Louis, AND JJ?”

PETE

“Were you able to speak with Connie concerning JJ?”

“She’s not ready.”

PHILLIP CHAPMAN

"Connie, Doug was able to purchase Magic."

"Yes, I'm so happy because I know he will be well cared for."

"I just spoke with Doug, and his purchase of Magic was actually through a conglomerate created for the purpose of keeping Magic on the race circuit. Doug is principal owner, but the rest own a percentage and will recoup their investment through his winnings."

"I have mixed feelings towards that Phillip. I'm torn between him racing and not racing. I mean, I want only the best for Doug, and of course, Magic, but I might not be able to afford to buy him back. That was part of my reasoning behind the sale to Doug. I hoped to keep him close, close enough to regain ownership. Do you know his schedule?"

"No, not for certain, but I do know Doug mentioned California."

AMANDA BORDILLON

"Uncle JJ, what's wrong? Do you wish you hadn't sold your business?" Amanda stands and walks to her uncle's location on the front porch. "No, it's more than that, isn't it? Your thoughts are in Oklahoma and the woman you met while you were checking on Charlie. Connie what? What is her last name? Tell me, and I'll call her. I can't stand seeing you like this. It's been months. Just call…whatever the misunderstanding, it can't be worth what you're going through. Whatever you did, just say you're sorry. If you're worried about me, don't be. After Momma's death, I was rocky for a little while, but whatever you promised Momma about taking care of me, I'm okay, believe me!"

JJ, not moving his gaze from the line of trees, thinks, *"No baby girl, my sole purpose of returning to California was liquidation of assets. Yes, liquidation and then returning to Oklahoma to rescue Connie. I'm man enough to say, "Connie, I'm sorry for leaving, so sorry." However, not man enough to tell you, dear niece, the whole truth concerning Connie and me. You have lost your Mother, and now...I, cannot, I just can't. I'm a man caught in the middle of two women I love but, I know it's only a matter of time. I hear the ticking, yes, ticking away in my head."* JJ, not realizing he's speaking aloud emphatically says, "Just do it!"

DETECTIVE DANIEL DOBBINS

"I just spoke with the Ministry of Defense and Ludlow has appeared before the magistrate where he signed the waiver of extradition back to our jurisdiction effective immediately."

PETE

"Hey, Sweetheart, only a few more hours before I get off and can't wait to see you. We will have to make this date last. Danny and I are going to France tomorrow, on the first international flight available, to bring Ludlow back for prosecution in the death of Cassie Walters."

"Connie, Pete and Danny left this morning to bring Ludlow back to stand trial."

"I know. I was a little surprised when I received a call from Detective Dobbins as almost all the information comes through you and Pete."

"Maybe the detective just felt you needed to know."

"That could be. He told me that he had been informed that the French implement company is fighting Ludlow for rights to a prototype for equipment to be used in the oil fields. Their petition claims Ludlow was still their employee while on leave of absence, that his prototype is legally theirs as it was developed through them."

"Does Danny believe it was originally Charles'?"

"He didn't go that far, as he believes that would be speculation on his part, but felt it would be to my benefit to bring the matter to my attorney's attention."

"Did you? Are you?"

"I haven't yet. Driscoll's firm is expensive not to mention their investigator. I wanted to spend any extra money on seeing Magic race. He's doing quite well, Rosie."

"That's wonderful. You must be proud as punch."

"A little of both, I'm proud for Magic, but his wins are pulling him further away from me. I'll never be able to reclaim him as each win elevates his standings and his value to his owners."

"Owners? I thought the trainer bought him."

"He did but had to bring in others to be able to purchase Magic at the auction as there were several bidders."

"I just wish you the best, Connie. I know you love that horse."

AMANDA BORDILLON

Amanda watches as a massive horse hauler pulls toward the stables. She heads to the back of the house as she hears the back door open. She sees Uncle JJ donning his hat, grabbing his sunglasses, and pulling his gloves from his back pocket as he opens the door to exit the sunroom.

He motions the driver to circle and park with the back of the hauler facing the portico area of the stables. As the semi makes the final turn, Amanda gasps as she notices the trailers state of registry. Oklahoma! Running forward, with every intention of confronting her uncle, Amanda stops short as she miraculously sees a wide-grinned smile on her uncle's face that she hadn't witnessed in all these long months now.

The driver exits to the warm welcome of JJ, and not missing a beat, he turns and says, "Doug, I would like you to meet my niece, Amanda Bordillon. Amanda, this is Doug Hartly."

JJ turns, as he and Doug advance to start the hydraulics that control the exit ramp. Amanda retreats to the far left so not to deter the process. Doug enters the trailer and proudly emerges with a smile that not only equals JJ's but even surpasses his.

As the beautiful stallion impressively starts his descent, Amanda's breath is taken away. Then after only a few steps into full view, the stallion stops, turns his gaze directly on Amanda, whinnies and shakes his head and glistening mane in assent of her presence.

"Right this way, Doug. I believe Magic will be most comfortable in this stall."

Amanda, now realizing she's glued in place, jumps and runs to catch up, as she's determined not to miss one word of this conversation.

"Doug, Magic looks like he made the trip well."

Doug answers JJ's query as he releases Magic into his stall, "Yes, no problems at all, but glad he will have a few down days to get acclimated."

Amanda, now alongside, starts to interject but isn't fast enough as JJ says, "What specifically do we need to do? Special rations?"

"No, I bring everything with me on the transport. There's an area dedicated to Magic's needs."

Amanda, now stepping forward, wanting to be included in the duo's circle, opens her mouth, only to be cut off by her uncle as he continues the dialogue.

"I have ranch hands employed who will be here momentarily and will be in residence in the bunkhouse area during your stay."

"Thanks, JJ, much appreciated."

Amanda will not be denied any further but as she begins to speak, the excitement of the moment causes her voice to crack and as she coughs in disbelief, JJ turns toward her and says, "Amanda,

Doug and I are co-owners of this beauty. Would you be so kind as to let us finish, and we will meet you at the house in a bit if you would like to provide some refreshments."

Amanda bristles at his surly dismissal, but now, firmly composed, she replies, "Of course." She nods in the direction of Doug as she retreats, wishing she had her boots on instead of flip-flops.

She busily bustles preparing sandwiches, tea, and lemonade while not wandering far from the large window that gives her sight of the stables.

Around the circular table under the large ceiling fan in the kitchen, Doug eagerly accepts his plate and drink. JJ offers Doug a room in the house as the bedrooms are numerous, but he declines saying the trailer has very nice accommodations for him.

Amanda, biding her time, finally notices a lull in the conversation toward the last of the sandwiches. Leaning forward towards the table, she states, "So, Mr. Hartly, have you….." only to be cut off in mid-sentence as the truck with the stable hands enters on the gravel road, and Doug and JJ both jump from their chairs.

Amanda starts to follow but decides just to pace the kitchen as she slams the remains of her refreshment effort into the refrigerator.

It seems like an eternity as she watches the day fade into evening, and evening fades into night before voices rise in farewell greetings. She sees her uncle advancing toward the house, and she vows not to be denied this time.

Now standing in the doorway directly in front of JJ, with legs apart and hands on hips, thus making herself have complete control of his entry, Amanda determinedly states in a convicting voice, "Enough is enough. What exactly happened in Oklahoma?"

JJ, with a defeated shake of his head, says, "Sit down, Amanda."

ROSIE REDMOND

"Connie, Pete has called me two and three times a day while he has been gone. He said he misses me something terrible, and he wants me to quit work. He said our hours do not match up well, and he didn't recognize my importance to him until we are not together, or something like that. And get this. He said we need to have a serious talk when he gets back. Are you thinking what I'm thinking? Oh, holy moly!"

DETECTIVE DANIEL DOBBINS

"Pete, where is your head. You certainly weren't in that meeting. I've never seen you like this. I thought you would be happy. No, change that to jumping with joy when I talked the captain into both of us making the trip. You're now an international traveler, so get a grip! We are going to have some down time, and I want to experience France and not worry about you. Pete, you hear me? Are you listening?"

TOP NEWS STORY

Oklahoma City, Oklahoma (CNN) Police Chief of the Oklahoma City Police Department announced at a news conference earlier today that Louis Ludlow has been extradited from Saveur, France to stand trial for the murder of Cassie Walters. He further stated that Ludlow was a person of interest in connection with the fall and subsequent death of Charles Sinclair.

DETECTIVE DANIEL DOBBINS

"Would you please state your full name?"

"Louis Leonard Ludlow."

"And Mr. Ludlow, you have been advised of your rights under the Miranda rights?"

"Yes."

"You also need to be advised that this interrogation is being recorded for possible playback at a later time and date which may or may not be advantageous to you. And you have, of your own free will, without any coercion, and of your own accord, agreed to speak with me without an attorney present?"

"Yes, I just want this over. I'm not a bad person, or I wasn't a bad person. I just found myself in circumstances that seemed to compound at every turn. Can't believe this all started as a little side venture. At the time, the investment appeared to present itself as a lucrative way to a possible early retirement. I gave Charles Sinclair my entire savings, but to be able to keep the profits just between the two of us, I needed more capital, so I, I…borrowed the rest from the company. I see now this all happened because I became greedy. My dad always said, be thankful for your God-given blessings, and son, don't get greedy. I should have stopped with my original investment but, I didn't, as Sinclair…."

Now, as he thought of Charles Sinclair's elaborate swindle, he began bowing his back and straightening his position in his chair, but the clank of the metal cuffs on the stainless steel table as he resisted his tether quickly jolted him back to his current position and took his futile fight from him.

"Continue, Mr. Ludlow."

"I checked the Los Angeles County Clerk's records to find out who owned the land on the oil lease site and was told there's no lease for the location I knew to be the Black Magic Oil site. I went to the estate in upper Los Angeles County but couldn't get any information from the girl there."

"So what's your connection to JJ Paige?"

"Who?"

"Jeremiah Jason Paige."

"Never heard of him. Is he the owner?"

With no comment to affirm or deny Ludlow's question, Detective Dobbins continues, "Let's visit a little more concerning Charles Sinclair."

"No, I need a rest. No, please."

"I'm sorry, but you have mistaken your position in this situation. This has nothing to do with your comfort nor with your needs and wants at this moment. No, this has to do with the truth, letting Sinclair's family have some closure and know why his widow finds herself alone."

Ludlow now animated, continues, "She was probably a part of the whole thing, but, somebody was looking out for me. After I hit that dead end at the California estate, a day at the track led me to his wife, her racehorse and the Oklahoma connection. She was very forthcoming, and that's when I made my trip to Oklahoma and…"

Ludlow continues reliving his experience in Oklahoma, the moment he almost believed his heart and had the opportunity to back his way out of the Sinclair residence as he envisioned the church in France where he felt God's presence. "If I'd only listened to my heart. We all have choices in life, and until now, I have chosen the right path." Ludlow attempts to move his hands, this time to his eyes to shield the tears from his oh-so-close accuser, but the clank of his cuffs is becoming an all too familiar sound that was eerily taunting him.

Detective Dobbins prods him unmercifully to continue and moves Ludlow ever so slowly, but oh so precisely, in the direction of the missing files.

"So you went to the Sinclair estate with the full intention of exacting revenge on Charles Sinclair?"

"No, no, not at all. I was just going to talk to him and try to get some idea of when I could get all or even just part of my money back."

"So, when did you get possession of Sinclair's computer files?"

Ludlow, not showing any shock or concern over the detective's question, answers with a chuckle, "That took quite a little detective work," Ludlow replied, not realizing how ironic his statement was.

He continues and even credits Cassie with putting him in a situation in which he had to become familiar with the flash drive that he used to download the files from Sinclair's computer.

My maneuvering paid off! There it is, the statement that connects all three. Charles Sinclair, the missing files and Cassie Walters. Therefore, the prototype does belong to Connie Sinclair. Now, Detective Dobbins leans into the wall, in his usual position while in the interrogation room, looks at the camera in the corner, and lets himself enjoy this one rare shift in behavior by displaying a Cheshire cat smile.

PETE

"Just landed. We are transporting Ludlow to Oklahoma County Jail, and after he's booked, I'll head your way. What do you mean you're still at work? Didn't you quit, or are you working through your two-week notice? Okay, I could use some sleep, so call me when you leave work. You'll still be off at 2, right?"

ROSIE REDMOND

"Connie, he's back."

"That's good."

"You'd think so, right?'

"Rosie, are you okay. Is something wrong? You were so happy, and I might add, confident when I spoke with you last."

"I don't know. This whole thing is just all so…so different now."

"At police headquarters, during interrogation, you were flirting like crazy with him. I remember distinctly, sitting forward to get a better view of your face and making sure the dripping-with-honey words were coming out of your mouth. Now, you don't know. What is so different? You don't like Pete anymore?"

"I just don't know. I keep going through full circles in my mind. You know how I have a tendency to roll things back and forth in my head; well, I'm past rolling, I have a full-blown battle in my head. But, you're right. This was all fun, and I was relishing all the flirting. Now, life's getting real and getting there real fast. Just a few days ago I said, "Be careful and see ya, when he left for the airport, to now quitting my job and him wanting to have an adult conversation when we see each other later tonight. Is this another bridge I shouldn't cross?

Connie, you there? Man, oh man. You have a way of just tuning people out. Connie, I need you to be here for me!"

"I'm here, Rosie, and I'm here for you, now. What you just said was ringing in my ears. Is this another bridge I shouldn't cross? Rosie, you know how I love Patsy Cline, and when she's on the radio, my hand goes up, and no one talks when Miss Patsy sings?"

Rosie, now chuckling, says, "Yup, I remember. You almost wore that CD out along with wearing me out. No offense, Miss Patsy, if you're listening."

"Rosie, I can't find a day I'm not lonely, a day I don't have memories echoing in my mind. There's just Miss Patsy and me on the radio and both of us crying, 'I want to be back in my baby's arms.' Don't do that Rosie. Please don't miss something that will make your life whole, rock you to your core, and leave you breathless as you thank God for bringing him into your life. Rosie, I feel Charles' presence as I spoke those words."

"Connie, I need you. I need your hug. I need your faith."

PETE

"Danny, I don't know."

"You don't know what. I didn't realize we were in a conversation. Did I miss something here? I'm working on the report. What are you doing?"

"Danny, I just spoke with Rosie, and she was at work."

"Afraid I don't see the problem!"

"While we were in France, I missed her something awful. I mean, my heart ached, I missed her so bad."

"Pete, you never said anything. I knew you seemed distant, but I never dreamed...uh, I mean, not that you aren't a good catch or anything, but I just never saw the two of you together." Danny, knowing he's being a little sarcastic says, "Doesn't she get to you with all that ‘rolling things through her mind’ stuff?”

Pete immediately taking the statement as a compliment, says, “Yeah, she does. She just has a way of thinking things through, doesn’t she? Thanks, Danny for bringing me back to my senses.”

ROSIE REDMOND

"Hello Pete, I'm home. I know it's only nine. I couldn't work with all this on my mind. Were you asleep? Good, glad I didn't wake you, but really wish you could have some time to be rested before we talk."

"Rosie, this is JJ."

"Boy, this has been one busy night for phone calls. I haven't had time to think one clear thought to myself."

"I'm sorry, should I call back? Or even better, you call me when you're able to talk. Don't worry about the time difference, just call."

"There's another thing. Do you know France is seven hours ahead of us, so sometimes when I talked to Pete, it was the next day? I had trouble figuring what time it was here to know what time it was there. I tell you, JJ, it's too much to think over. Life is getting way too complicated by my thinking; that's if, like I said, I still can find time to think about it."

JJ now feeling a little perplexed. "Okay, I think I understood that. Call me when you can talk."

Rosie, now walking in a circle in her small apartment, answers, "No, that's what I'm doing. Let's talk. You want Connie's number? You got her number, don't you, or did it get deleted? Guess I never told you that I tried to ask Connie if she was open to talking to you, but…well…I never asked her."

JJ, now unsettled. "You didn't? Rosie, I thought you were going to try and help me, I mean, help us?"

"Pete was here when I called, and she was having an 'oh woe is me, pity party.' I told her I had something to tell her concerning you but didn't want to hurt her any more than she was already hurting. JJ, there's dead silence, and when she finally came back, I heard her take a deep breath and then she said, I don't know, I actually don't know! You have hurt her something awful, JJ. I'm getting mad at you, just remembering that conversation and the sound of her voice. What is wrong with you?"

PETE

"Rosie, open the door, you have me concerned."

Rosie, with her hands cupping her nose and mouth, takes a deep long breath, glances in the hall mirror, and rubs the black smears from under her eyes. She knows that they must have appeared while talking to JJ, and when she almost cried, remembering Connie's voice at the mention of JJ's name. What a roller coaster this evening has been. So much emotionally happening between four people, and no opportunity to think. Just think it through. While still looking at her image in the mirror, she thinks, *"JJ and Connie should be together."* Then, *"Lord, oh Lord, why can't I be that decisive in my life?"*

"Rosie?"

While unlocking the door, she says, "I'm here, Pete. Come in," as she turns and walks in the other room.

Pete stops short and surveys the entry way and kitchen to his right. He steps left into the hall and glances into both bedrooms and bath. *"Could there be someone else here? Shake this feeling off, Pete. This is just your lack of sleep and cop mentality that has you on edge. But what's up with Rosie? When I left for France, she couldn't keep her hands off me, hanging on my arm at every opportunity, especially when we were out. Where's this shy behavior coming from? She hasn't even made eye contact, much less approach me."*

Slowly entering the living area, Pete glances both directions as he resists the urge to feel the gun holstered on his side. What could be causing these feelings? He now focuses his attention on Rosie, seated on the couch, and gets a moment of déjà vu as she sits shoeless, once more, and the only things gracing her feet are bright red toes and an ankle bracelet. Without a word, he seats himself on her right.

With a heavy sigh, Rosie glances his way, then looks at her feet to see if something was amiss. "Pete, we need to talk."

Pete, still feeling a little unsettled says, "That's why I'm here, and I'm ready to hear what you have to say."

Rosie thinks to herself, "*What exactly do I have to say? I haven't had time to think all this through. I need mind time!*"

Rosie catches him staring at her feet, as she self-consciously pulls them under her, which only shortens the distance between them and presses her to his side. In the moment it takes for them to make eye contact, they are in each other's arms in a ravenous kiss, lacking all self-control.

DOUGLAS HARTLY

As Doug exits the tack room, he stops to observe Amanda at Magic's stall as she strokes Magic's neck and Magic nuzzles her. Amanda's long shiny ebony hair almost disappears against the black of Magic's coat. As Doug's gaze continues downward, he gives a quick smile as he notices her boots and the missing flip flops she wore the night they first met. Advancing his gaze back up, Doug is drawn to the ribbons hanging loosely in her left hand, the color of her blue shirt. His eyes linger for only a mere moment at her tiny belted waist before workers entering the east door abruptly interrupt his thoughts. As he's shocked back to the reality of the moment, Doug notices the workers have also ceased their pace as they glance at each other as if interrupting some private moment between two people. Doug wonders, "*How long have I been stopped dead in my tracks? People all around but I'm only aware of one person, and my rapid heartbeat.*"

DETECTIVE DANIEL DOBBINS

"Mrs. Sinclair, Louis Ludlow admitted during interrogation, his involvement in your husband's death. Charges will be filed through the Canadian County District Attorney's Office. I have spoken with Assistance District Attorney Hannigan. She has informed me, after reviewing our report, the gravity and depth of charges to be filed will soon be determined."

Connie, sitting at the kitchen desk, grabs pen and paper. "Thank you so much for calling."

The detective continues, "I believe, in the heat of the moment, Ludlow pushed Mr. Sinclair."

Connie gives a relieved sigh. "I'm so thankful that the circumstances surrounding Charles' death are now known."

"I knew you would be. A couple of other things I would like to share. I think this determination will make a difference in any insurance settlement you received, so please have your lawyers look into that."

Connie, remembering her last conversation with her attorney, states, "I haven't received any compensation from insurance. Mr. Driscoll advised that several items had inadvertently missed being placed in the trust and are being handled through the Will clause. I'll notify him. Thanks so much."

"The last item of which you need to be aware pertains to the prototype to manufacture oil site equipment. Ludlow went into great depth as to the difficulty he encountered to gain entry to your computer. I don't know the procedure you need to take to reclaim the rights to this item. The process might just be a mere writ through the courts, or the files might be considered evidence and out of your reach until the trial ends. But I'm confident Mr. Driscoll is already handling this because of your prior contact on the matter when we spoke previously."

Connie, knowing she has opted not to incur any further expense with the law firm, states, "Thank you, Detective Dobbins." as she presses the red disconnect circle.

ROSIE REDMOND

"Is this actually happening? Am I to become Mrs. Peter...?

Hello, I was just starting to call. I know. I feel the same way. I woke up this morning and pinched myself to make sure I was awake. No, no date as of yet. I'm going slow and savoring every moment. I agree! Life is so short, and that's why I'm trying just to be in this one moment. I can't imagine life being much better than right now."

DRISCOLL AND DRISCOLL
Attorneys at Law

"Mrs. Sinclair, this is Deidra Hulbert, Investigator with Driscoll and Driscoll. We met briefly at the meeting at our offices earlier this year."

"Yes, Miss Hulbert, I remember. What can I do for you?"

"Mrs. Sinclair, the firm has been contacted by an implement company headquartered in France. They are requesting a meeting with you in the near future in reference to a set of design plans. These plans are for a prototype to be utilized in the oil fields. Arthur sent their request to me as he was unable to make any determination other than the prototype had been mentioned in your previous meeting. The company does business in the United States and stresses their availability isn't a problem."

"I see."

Deidra Hulbert continues, “Would you please get back with me, at your earliest convenience, on an appropriate date fitting your schedule?”

Connie without hesitation, remembering her stance on being in control of her situations, says, “Miss Hulbert, that won’t be necessary. Please forward all correspondence to my home address.”

“Mrs. Sinclair, this could become very laborious, not to mention legally entangled. I’m sure the partners would prefer that this is handled through the firm.”

Connie, with strength of voice, says, “I appreciate their concern, but I prefer the present documents and any future documents you receive, be forwarded immediately to me. You know, just go ahead and email me the corporate information now. Please include their contact number.”

Diedra Hulbert in a lower tone, “Certainly.”

“Miss Hulbert.”

“Yes.”

"There's a matter the firm can handle for me. I would appreciate, also, if this could be handled expeditiously."

"Certainly, how may we help?"

Connie, states, after changing her position hoping to stave off any detrimental feelings, "I have been informed that felony charges are to be filed in the death of Mr. Sinclair, and this could precipitate a change in Charles' life insurance. Would you see if this will be addressed?"

"I'll make certain this is brought to Arthur's attention immediately, along with what we have discussed."

"Thank you so much, Miss Hulbert. You have a good day."

"You also, Mrs. Sinclair."

AMANDA BORDILLON

"When does he race? You know, I want to be included," Amanda asks while closing the cabinet door.

JJ glances up and states, "Of course, you can be included, babe. You've completely gotten into this, haven't you?"

"Yes, I have. I was too young to appreciate the horses when we had them before. I didn't think so, but I now miss them."

"You were all into the riding part back then," JJ, giving a chuckle as the memory enters his mind. "We might be able to remedy the horse shortage."

"Magic is just so beautiful. When I'm with Doug, and he's putting him through his time trials, I can imagine Magic in flight as his mane and tail seem almost to lift him from the ground."

JJ straightens in his chair and asks, “You’re not bothering Doug when he’s working Magic, are you?”

Amanda now turns to face JJ. “I don’t think so. Has he said something to you to make you ask?”

“No, certainly not.”

Amanda, turning and looking toward the stables, decides she might ask Doug herself.

"I need to find a release. Go for a drive?

Constance thinks aloud while opening the door, *"Walk the garden? No, I feel like kicking that brick border. Oh Lord, Lord, Lord!"*

"I need to be on Magic's back and feel his power. That's exactly what I need. That's how I used to handle this restless feeling, by finding release through Magic."

"Hello, Phillip, would you give me Doug's number?"

JEREMIAH JASON PAIGE

As JJ enters the stables, he looks at Magic and says, "You're one beautiful animal. Guess the help I hired are earning their pay because you seem as if you have been buffed and polished to perfection."

JJ glances over his shoulder and sees Doug in the far corner on his phone. "I'm going to leave you and go have a chat with your friend. Will that be okay?" Magic lifts his head and gives a soft whinny as JJ turns and walks towards the far end of the barn.

JJ keeps a polite distance but does manage to hear Doug say, "I can't wait to see you and so good to hear your voice."

JJ, turns his back away from Doug, gives an "atta boy" chuckle and kicks the straw next to his boots. *Doug ole boy, you have a girlfriend!*

"Hey, JJ. Sorry, I didn't know you were here. You're never going to guess who that was just now."

"If I have to guess, I'd say your girlfriend from that smile on your face. Is she in Oklahoma?"

"Oh…no, not my girlfriend, but she's in Oklahoma and headed out here to watch Magic race!"

"Really?" JJ still displaying his wide grin.

"Yup, you remember me telling you that Magic's previous owner was unable to retain him and the circumstances upon which I obtained Magic?"

JJ's grin fades to a smile, before disappearing totally.

AMANDA BORDILLON

Amanda sits in the sunroom, waiting for an opportunity to speak with Doug, but only workers appear at any of the entrances of the stables. The afternoon wears on as the constant pitch of the cicadas confirms the heat of the day has arrived. She hears movement on the gravel drive and turns to see if this is JJ returning. He was gone when she got up this morning, and she was a little surprised as he usually gives her a heads-up before leaving the ranch. But, that's not necessary now. That was before the ranch had all this activity and she would have been alone. Yes, she's right, JJ's truck pulls past, but he isn't stopping at the house, just the stables. He seems to be in a hurry as he quickly enters with something and then leaves without a glance her direction. "Strange behavior, I must say. Wonder what that's all about?"

Amanda now stands and decides to abandon her post as late afternoon has advanced well into evening. As she closes the sunroom door behind her, she hears voices and recognizes one as Doug's.

Ha, ha, I was just giving up a minute too soon, she thinks as she runs toward the sounds of conversation. "Doug, may I speak with you a moment?"

"Sure, what's up?"

"Well, JJ and I were having a conversation and…"

"Amanda, come in and let me wash up a little, won't you?"

Doug opens the aluminum screen door for her while she maneuvers the two metal steps. As she enters what could only be described as a very nice RV, she thinks, *who would have imagined all of this in a horse hauler.*

To her right is a regular size sofa, soft gray in color. Immediately in front is a love seat of matching fabric and to her left are two chairs in a gray, silver and yellow fabric. Behind the chairs, she sees the kitchen with stainless steel appliances, which appears to be full size. Past that and down a short hall must be the bed and bath, as Doug heads that direction after he asks her to be seated.

She decides to sit in one of the chairs, which is being basked in the soft glow of the lamp. Upon crossing her legs, she notices Doug has removed his boots and set them by the door on a small mat. No wonder this place looks so new. Glancing at her feet, she thinks, *"I could have placed my shoes there also as I'm in flip flops again. I need to wear boots more often. You'd think I don't have any. Really!"*

Doug seems to be taking an inordinate amount of time as she hears the sound of soft music coming through the speakers above the love seat, followed by a very pleasing aroma of men's cologne. He has gotten cleaned up for me! No more than the time it takes her thought to mature into a warm feeling, she hears Doug behind her and the jingle of ice in a glass. *Oh no. He's fixing drinks.* At that moment, Doug enters her view and says, "I've already downed two glasses of water, and I've brought you one."

"Where is my mind going with this?" Amanda admits she has lead a sheltered life, as the solitude of the ranch is none too conducive to meeting people her age.

"This is very comfy, and to think JJ was afraid you would be uncomfortable not sleeping in the house."

Doug smiles but doesn't answer, as he's wondering why Amanda has suddenly dropped 'uncle' from JJ's name

"He has been gone all day. Do you have any idea what he might be doing?" Amanda queries. "Well, no matter. I haven't fixed supper."

Amanda realizes she's the only one in conversation, turns in her chair to see if Doug is still awake. Yes, he's awake and looking quite handsome in her estimation.

He leans up and places his glass on the lamp table while he takes hers as she gently releases the glass to his control, and says, "May I have this dance?"

CONSTANCE LOUISE SINCLAIR

"This feels good, really, really good. I should have done this earlier," Connie thinks, as she stands at the luggage carousel. Usually, Charles would be waiting for me as I exit this area, but that season of my life is to be no more. Where has the time gone? So much water under the bridge. The proverbial bridge that Rosie is scared to cross. Now Rosie has not only crossed that bridge but jumped in, swam around and even under. Rosie has never thought love would come her way. Not just love, but complete, wholehearted, gut wrenching love. Love, that God, in his divine wisdom, has freely lavished and ordained upon his children. Yes, from the dawning of time and before, God has had a plan that we should not be alone. He made Adam and quickly joined him to Eve. When I return to Oklahoma, the fun will begin, as there's a wedding to help plan.

"Ma'am, didn't you say your luggage had multicolored ribbons on them?"

"Oh, yes, thanks so much."

"Here, please allow me."

"Thank you, Sir."

"Charles you were right. You always said I needed a keeper," Connie thinks silently, as she rolls one and carries the other piece of luggage while she tries to keep her bag on her shoulder. *Oh great! A down escalator! This is going to be interesting.*

DOUGLAS HARTLY

"Hello, Connie. I'm thrilled you're here. Did you have a good flight?"

"Oh Doug, I'm elated to be here. I should have done this long ago. This just feels so liberating. I have almost been in a self-imposed prison at the estate without realizing that until now."

"Well, we're certainly glad you're here."

"Oh yes, you and Magic. I can't wait."

"Yes, Magic also. However, he's being stabled at my partner's ranch in upper Los Angeles County. Their generosity has been a godsend for Magic not to have to be rousted to numerous locations not to mention training sites."

"How is he, Doug? I know, from all reports he's being touted as the black stallion that actually deserves his name."

"I know Connie. Everyone says he's pure magic to watch on the track. You couldn't have given him a more deserving name."

As they both laugh and continue their long awaited conversation, the miles pass quickly until…

"We're here, Connie. Do you want to get settled in your room at the house or see Magic first?"

"You have to ask?"

"Magic, it is."

Connie enters the barn and sees Magic at the far end of his stall. She taps the gate, and as Magic turns, she says, "Oh Magic, come here, my sweet boy."

Magic, with a soft whinny of consent, nuzzles the one missing part of his life for far too many months as unabated tears of joy run from Connie's eyes. "I have missed you so much. I know, I know," Connie says, as the long-awaited reunion unfolds.

AMANDA BORDILLON

Amanda steels herself for the event ahead. She keeps checking the mirror as sleep has evaded her for several reasons last night. How could this be happening after the delightful time with Doug? Dancing in his arms was like a fairy tale come true. She's ashamed to admit she has never been held by a man in that type of embrace. No, up until now, she has only danced on the toes of her uncle, and yes, on the boots of Charlie as he and Momma twirled her between them. How has she been so cheated out of life; out of knowing a father as other children know a true father? No matter, she has long ago come to terms with that. Yes, she even has come to terms with the realization of Charles Sinclair as her father. However, this, also, wasn't to be. She shudders as she remembers the terrible, horrible things she said to him the last time they were together. He died not knowing she was sorry. He would never know she was so, so sorry.

Just a few short hours ago, as she and Doug danced the evening away, they laughed as he pulled her toward him. During the night, if she lived in anyone else's world, she would be remembering his smell, his smile, his touch, while she lay in bed. No, today's reality is her world, and her world will have to include the meeting that is yet to come.

DOUGLAS HARTLY

"Connie, there's someone I want you to meet."

Connie turns and says, "Yes, I'm anxious to meet him also."

"Well, he's not here right now, and I do want you to meet him, but…"

"But what Doug, what is wrong?"

"Oh Connie, no, there's nothing wrong. No, to the contrary, there's something quite right. Well, at least, in my eyes there's something right, and I'm hoping in her eyes, also." Now patting Magic on his muscular neck as he chuckles, "Magic has been quite busy at match-making."

"Douglas Hartly!" Connie exclaims as she tightly hugs his neck. "Who is she? When do I get to meet her? How long have you known? I want every detail." Connie backs a couple of steps and leans into Magic's stall gate and with crossed arms softly says, "I just love watching people experience love, especially when they're experiencing love for the first time. There's nothing like the moments of the first touch and the first in-depth conversation where your eyes are locked and nothing else, at that moment, exists except the two of you. I'm just happy beyond words."

"I am, too, Connie! I am, too! You know how hard dating is on the circuit. You can't have any life much less consider dating. You're at the track almost non-stop, or you're on the road in route to the next event. I'd given up hope of ever even envisioning myself in this position, but I think love is finally within my reach."

"Tell me more!"

"Gladly. I've had no one to talk to out here. Magic brought us together. She has loved him from the first time she watched him in a timed trial and never, from that moment, missed being near him. I came out of the tack room a few weeks back, saw her with Magic, and I knew, just knew. I felt this tingle from head to toe and was just lost in the moment."

"You're making me tingle now. I love 'love'."

"Her name is Amanda, and you're going to meet her in a moment as this is her ranch. She has graciously invited you to stay here instead of in a hotel, so you and Magic can have more time together."

"She sounds charming."

"Well, let's head to the house. You can meet her and get settled," Doug states as he helps Connie in the truck.

The short distance was without conversation as all Connie could do was smile and shake her head as two special people in her life have now found love. She knows she will be attending both weddings, Rosie's and now Doug's.

AMANDA BORDILLON

Amanda hears the doors slam and Doug start the truck. "I can do this. I can do this," now walking in circles. "I have to do this, if only for Doug. He's surely the one, Lord. Please let this be real. Please, sweet Jesus!"

"Come on in, Connie. Amanda is usually in the sunroom when she hears me coming. Amanda?"

"Yes, I'm here."

"Amanda, this is Connie Sinclair, Magic's previous owner. Connie, I'll grab your luggage."

"Come in. So nice to meet you. Let's go inside where the air is a little cooler."

"Thank you. I appreciate you letting me stay while I'm visiting Magic. Doug said you're quite taken with Magic, also."

Amanda's face lights up as she revisits her attendance at the timed trials and her vision of Magic in flight. Connie can see Amanda's love for Magic is real. The women get on quite well, and Amanda can hardly believe that she feels that Connie indeed seems pleasant.

As Connie continues in conversation, Amanda watches her mannerisms, the way she flips her blonde hair to one side as she laughs, the way she holds her head and how her mouth curls before displaying her most charming smile. Yes, Connie Sinclair is charming.

Connie now leaning forward, states, "The thing that brought me here was remembering the feel of power as I rode Magic. Don't you think he has a gait like no other?"

Amanda, looking a little perplexed, says, "I've never ridden him. I don't think anyone can now, as Magic's standings have risen to such a level, making riding economically unfeasible."

"I guess you're right. I hate to say this, but Magic is performing for Doug like never before. I'm so proud for Magic. He deserves every win."

Doug entering from the back of the house says, "You're all set. I'm heading back to the stable."

Connie, glancing Amanda's way, looks as if she's requesting approval from Amanda to go back with Magic. "You wouldn't mind, would you, if I go with Doug?"

"Certainly not, Mrs. Sinclair."

"Amanda, please call me Connie. I'm sorry, I don't even know your last name."

Doug says, "Please accept my apologies. Amanda's last name is Bordillon, Amanda Bordillon!"

CONSTANCE LOUISE SINCLAIR

Now back with Magic, Connie girds herself to maintain control. Control of her body, her emotions, and her need to…to escape! Yes run, run until she can run no more. To be in a different place, a place where she can sort through this. Up until this moment, Bordillon has just been a location in California where…where what? "*Has Charles been here? Certainly, he has. Deidra Hulbert said the Bordillon Ranch is where the bulk of the money has been funneled. Who is Amanda? How can you be married to a man and not know…But know what?*" Connie settle down, you're going in circles. "Oh Lord, what else could happen on this much needed leisurely trip? Oh, Magic, sweet Magic."

"Hello, Connie," JJ says as he walks her way.

Connie goes rigid and does not attempt to turn his direction.

JJ halts, "I know this must be a shock for you." His statement receives nothing but silence. He stands and waits for some acknowledgment of his presence. Nothing comes. "Connie. Connie, please." Still, the only sound is from Connie's sweet Magic.

JJ turns and leaves.

Addressing JJ and Amanda at the house after exhaling a deep breath, Doug says, “I’ve come for Connie’s things.”

JJ, now stands, says, “She’s leaving?”

“No, but I did a lot of talking to get her settled down before I could even start to convince her this time of day is late to leave. Even if she had demanded to be taken to the airport, there’s no way I, with a clear conscience, would leave her in her condition. She‘s staying in the RV.”

JJ starts toward the bedroom and says, “I’ll help you.”

“No, I can manage, but I’ll be back to bunk here.”

Doug glances Amanda’s way. She sits in the corner, silent and still. A tissue box rests beside her and crumpled tissues in her lap. What has happened? What could have driven three people into such a morose state of mind? Doug's heart aches for her, as he controls his impulse to go and comfort her.

Upon gathering the luggage, he sets them in the hall and entering the living room, sternly looks at JJ and says, "I expect you to be ready to talk when I return."

JJ nods assent.

JEREMIAH JASON PAIGE

JJ meets Doug in the sunroom upon hearing the door open. Their talk continues into the early hours of the morning. Long after Doug has gone to bed, JJ continues his vigil, never taking his eyes off the trailer and the figure that's constantly in motion. JJ thinks, *"In motion like a trapped animal. Oh Lord, what have I done?"*

AMANDA BORDILLON

Late into the morning, Amanda finds JJ asleep in the sunroom. Without hesitation, she roughly awakens him. With arms crossed, tissues wadded in her hands and foot tapping the floor, she exclaims, “Fix this; you have to fix this! I like her. I don’t know if I was expecting to or not, but I do. I like her!”

JEREMIAH JASON PAIGE

Showered, coffee in hand, JJ stands at the sunroom door gazing at the windows, where just hours before, Connie paced like a trapped animal. Could he do this? Could he "fix this?"

"Lord, I need your help. Give me the words," JJ softly prays as he heads her way. He glances back at the house and sees Amanda at the kitchen window deftly shaking her head from side to side as her glare reminds him of all that's at stake. He then remembers the package he had placed in the stable's office and diverts his steps in that direction.

Standing only a few short feet from Connie but actually a million miles, JJ knocks.

The door opens immediately, but Connie isn't there. Has she been expecting him or has she been watching him from afar?

He steps in and sees her standing in the kitchen. No longer her back to him, he realizes the months upon months he has gone without seeing her face. She too is dressed with luggage beside her. So she's leaving. As he returns to her eyes, he's surprised by her control as she says, "Sit down, JJ."

"Okay, I will, but please sit in a chair, also."

"I'm fine, thank you," she dryly answers. "You be seated, though." Her words have a harsh grating tone.

"Connie, I would like to explain. You see…."

"No explanation needed. I've spoken with Doug, and I think he has conveyed to me the parts of the story…No, he has conveyed to me the parts of my LIFE to which I obviously have been oblivious. Connie, now turning, walks to the end of the bar, and says, "But there's something you can answer."

"Anything. Connie, please sit down."

Her determination to stand remains evident. "How could you leave me as I sat in jail? How could you just desert me?"

JJ counters, "I had so much in my head. I knew they were seriously looking at me for the murder of that girl. I knew I'd been with you under false pretenses, and you had no idea of my identity. I knew I had to find some way to tell Amanda I was in love with her father's wife, and all this just after she had lost her Mother, my sister. But Connie, most of all, I knew I had to try and raise the money to return to Oklahoma and save you from total annihilation. And I tried, Connie, I so tried. I sold my business and turned all my holdings into cash, but that took time. Time I didn't have as the sale happened before I could gather the funds.

I often spoke with Rosie and Pete, and they kept me advised on your circumstance. I even asked her to tell you I wanted to talk to you. Didn't she tell you?"

"Yes, yes, she did. But why didn't you just call me? You had my number."

"I know, I know I did. When I got to that point, I found out Magic was in California." At this time in the conversation at the mention of Magic, Connie turns toward the sink to shield her emotion from JJ as he continues, "And I had the opportunity and the funds to become co-owner."

Connie directs her gaze out the kitchen window in an effort to disconnect herself and her raw feelings from the conversation. She's now finished in all aspects of the word. She notices movement at the house and sees Amanda entering the sunroom. Her feelings immediately soften as she states, "That beautiful girl is Charles' child? You know, we were unable to have a child."

"Yes, I know. Amanda is Charlie's and my sister's child. We knew him as Charlie and Amanda was in awe of him. I wish you could have seen her when Charlie would drive up. She would just become ecstatic." JJ quickly reels himself in, as he cannot imagine what Connie was going through. "Connie, Amanda is so upset. She likes you, and she's alone, so alone."

Connie turns and makes, for the first time, complete and telling eye contact with JJ. "Doug is here to take me to the airport."

"Is there anything I can say? Any way to convince you to stay just for one more day?" He sees her answer in her eyes without a word being spoken.

JJ lowers his head, and seeing the package in his hand, says, "Connie, this is for you. This is papers to Magic or at least my share in Magic. They are all signed and notarized. I wasn't in time to come and save you in Oklahoma, but the money was enough to get Magic partially back for you."

"Oh JJ, love isn't having money or possessions. Love is being there for all time. You know, rich or poor, sickness or health, the GOOD, and BAD, through the thick and thin of life. I'm not sure if you understand any of that."

Doug enters as she walks past.

CONSTANCE LOUISE SINCLAIR

"Yes, this is Constance Sinclair, and I see you returned my call while I was out of state. Thank you, I'll hold."

"Mrs. Sinclair, I'm so glad to speak with you finally. Sorry, we have missed each other the past couple of times. I, or we the company, were wondering if you had made any decision about our offer to build the prototype, at our expense, of course. We will want documentation that states that we will be the sole manufacturer for the sale of the equipment to any and all users if the prototype proves to be advantageous in the oil fields. But, I can tell you every expert that has been a part of this process, sees nothing that could prevent this from working."

Connie then counters, "And I retain all patents and any future production revenues?"

"Yes, that's correct."

"One other thing. I know this has not been discussed, but I'm now open to the prototype being used on my wells first. I've become aware that I'll have more free time to be involved."

"I see no problem in that. The papers will be to you within the week."

DOUGLAS HARTLY

"Amanda, are you here?" Doug inquires, before knocking on the sunroom door once more.

"Yes, I'm here. Come in."

Doug, now in a concerned tone, says, "You haven't been at the last couple of trials for Magic. I just was wondering…"

Amanda, now entering the kitchen, glances his way. "Come on in. Could I offer you something?"

"Tea would be great. Thanks." Doug stands with his hat in his hand as he watches Amanda fix their drinks and place cookies on a plate. He realizes that he doesn't feel comfortable enough to casually take a seat without being invited, even though they had shared that one special evening. He, with hand to his mouth, realizes that was the only time he had felt her touch. Would that be the last? That one night which now seems an eternity ago, Oh Lord, how could things that seem so right turn suddenly, suddenly what? He is going to say turn so wrong, but as he stands looking at her, he could never use that word in his thoughts toward her.

Amanda turns, and they make eye contact. She flushes, and her once stern face shows the smallest twitch of the beginning of a smile. "Please sit down, Doug. You were saying?"

"As I was saying, you missed Magic's trials, and I just was concerned."

"No need. I guess I wasn't sure of your thoughts," she replies as she shakes her head.

"My thoughts?"

"Your thoughts on this whole situation." Amanda, now lowering her head, continues. "Doug, you literally learned of my entire life in three short hours. From birth to this moment in time, and that being after your good friend was demoralized in your presence. What must you think of me? Think of us?"

Doug barely letting the last word of her sentence leave her lips before he cups her hand in his. He's thankful that he receives no resistance and feels only the warmth of her hand. "I know, Amanda. Everything was going wonderfully. Magic is coming along at an incredible pace, and I give you credit for that as he runs his heart out for you. I believe Magic's improved behavior has to do with seeing you cheering him on at the rails at the trials. I not only speak for Magic, but I've missed seeing you, also," Doug states as he softly gives her hand a gentle squeeze. "As for the circumstances of the other evening, I'm sorry if I appeared overly concerned for Connie, but this was so unexpected, just so out-of-the-norm of anything I would have dreamed happening." Doug, now with a softer voice, says, "Please, Amanda, accept my apologies if I led you to believe I was in any way upset with you."

Amanda, turns her head and tries to halt a tear from falling, but realizes it's too late, says, "When you think about us, no better words could have been spoken as we truly are out-of-the-norm. Oh, Doug, I should be apologizing, not only to you but also to my whole family. If you can call what we had a family. I never knew our life was different from anyone else because this is all I knew. I feel so used. Not in the mistreated sense of the word, but used, wasted, exhausted. I'm just exhausted, exhausted all the way to the core of who I am, or who I thought I was, or ever hope to be!"

Doug, knowing he has no momentary answer for a girl consumed by years of lies, sits silently. Then, without further thought, he does the only thing in his power at this moment, and that's to offer some comfort as he moves his chair closer to Amanda and she lays her head on his shoulder.

JEREMIAH JASON PAIGE

"Rosie, I've messed this up," JJ says in a forlorn voice.

"Messed up what?"

JJ, now trying to decide if she doesn't know or is just pretending, says, "You haven't spoken with Connie?"

"No, she's in California watching Magic win some races, and she said she didn't know how long she would be gone. JJ, she has been so down in the dumps that I think she will come back a new person. You know, Connie is such a people person, hugging and all that. I've never been much of a hugger, you know, never big on people getting in my space and all, but Connie has changed all that. I'm open to a hug from her anytime. How can you not like a person as positive, open and honest as Connie?"

"JJ, you there? JJ??

ROSIE REDMOND

"Connie, this is Rosie. You're still in California, aren't you?" Rosie only hears Connie's muffled crying. "Honey, you stay put, I'll be right out!"

Rosie, now with Connie, says, “Go on, I’m still following you, honey. I got that part.”

“Oh Rosie, I’m just repeating myself, aren’t I? I’m just making no sense at all.”

“Well, you might be going a little in circles, but I’ve kept up pretty good with you. I must say if I wasn’t hearing this from your mouth, I would be inclined to question some of what you’ve told me. Man, oh man!”

Connie, as she wipes her eyes one last time, wonders if there could be anything that she’s left out, stands and walks to the fireplace where Magic’s portrait has, through the gracious acts of friends, been returned says, “You know who I feel so sorry for?”

Rosie bristles as she states, “No, better not be JJ.”

"No, not JJ, Doug," Connie says as she tries, uselessly, to un-wad a tissue. "He had just opened his heart to me concerning the girl of his dreams, and my thought was that two of my best friends are going to be happy. You and Doug."

"Oh, honey, you classify me as a best friend?"

Connie walks over to Rosie, and with eyes moist, states, "I most certainly do. Stand up and give me a hug."

Without a moment's hesitation, Rosie rises and welcomes Connie's embrace, while Connie, having Rosie in a full blown hug, says, "Who else would sit and listen for hours to my troubles?"

Rosie chuckles and says, "Not like this is the first time."

"Oh my, I'm so sorry, Rosie, you better go. Pete will be tired of waiting by now."

"Are you kidding, Honey? Pete left hours ago. You got me for the night. I'm just glad, this time, we didn't have to blow our nose on dirty cleaning rags!"

DETECTIVE DANIEL DOBBINS

"I've just been informed by Assistant District Attorney Hannigan that Louis Ludlow's attorney has advised her that Ludlow is open to taking a plea agreement in lieu of going to trial."

"What does that mean exactly, where Charles' death is concerned?"

"Ludlow will agree to a prearranged sentence in the Walters girl's death and will plead *nolo contendere* in Charles' death. But what needs to concern you is the *nolo contendere* part. That, in laymen's terms, means Ludlow neither agrees nor denies his involvement in Charles' death."

"But he told you he did!"

"Yes, he did, and that's why you need to voice your concern, as I well did earlier today because I'm not certain what implications that might have on your insurance policy payment."

"I see."

"I can tell you this. The question you need to ask the District Attorney is if she's certain the Judge will find in favor of the state in Charles' death. Also, will that be enough to prove other than accidental death with your insurance company?"

CONSTANCE LOUISE SINCLAIR

Now renewed by the morning's light and sleep, Connie says, "Rosie, thanks for rushing to my rescue last night. All-in-all, I've enjoyed our time together."

"You mean, our slumber party. This was fun, and your home is beautiful."

"Thank you, but you know, I would give it all back to have things return to happier times."

"I know you would, honey. But is there such a thing when men are concerned?" Rosie says with a chuckle.

"Rosie, you're so funny. How true is that? You know that phone call I had earlier was from a friend saying she went to bed in tears Saturday night over almost this same thing. Deep hurt at the hands of a man. I've made my mind up, right now and with you as my witness; I'll never let a man make me cry again. From now on, I'll be in control of my own circumstances. Take me for who I am and where I am in this season of my life. I'll walk tall and confident as I continue to reclaim my life, as well my friend should."

ROSIE AND PETE'S WEDDING

The day is beautiful; azure skies greet the guests as they arrive at the Sinclair Estate. Immediately upon entering the arched gates, both sides of the drive are adorned with hanging baskets every few feet. Under the portico, as guests arrive, valets quickly sweep their cars away to allow for the numerous others being welcomed.

The walkway now leads guests between the profusely lined hydrangea bushes. The double oversized entry doors stand open wide, and on each side and above is a stained glass of rose and turquoise. Inside the two-story tall marble-floored foyer, a large circular table stands graced by a large floral vase, which sits under a crystal chandelier.

Walking forward and immediately on the right, guests see the grand staircase with rails covered in floral and ivy tendrils. At the top of the stairs, directly in front of the landing, a much larger stained glass window that mirrors the front, draws their attention.

The other side of the massive room holds the fireplace surrounded by luxurious leather furnishings. A Tiffany fireplace screen in gold and greens with one centered red jewel and matching lamps further add to the decor. Live flower arrangements of hydrangea and roses are everywhere. The staff is serving drinks and *hors d'oeuvres* as guests mingle.

Ben, the cleaning crew supervisor and Rosie and Connie's former boss, tells his wife, "Can you believe I used to boss her around?" The others in the group chuckle and say, "Just glad we didn't have to ride out here in a police bus, as we did during the investigation."

Continuing toward the garden, guests enter the Sunroom/Gallery, filled with oils, pastels, and watercolor paintings. Live orchids at the far end are displayed on mirrored shelves, which only accentuate their beauty. On the far wall, a large oversized settee in crème linen with toile pillows and more stained glass lighting are set in a most welcoming manner.

Upon turning right, the guests are led to the verandah with a full open-air kitchen on the north end, being most efficiently manned, as food is prepared. More flowers are in abundance as everyone quickly becomes aware of Connie's love of flowers.

The garden with the grape arbor, which is perpetually lit, is further adorned with flowers, candles, and ivy to enhance the late afternoon wedding. In front are lines of white chairs with ivy tendrils and flowers on each chair, and at the center and end aisles.

The large white tents are visible past the seating, as guests are tempted by the smell of smoked ribs, brisket, chicken, and sausages. Anything that could be smoked is on the menu tonight, as the caterer is known for the numerous parties he has served at the Sinclair Estate.

The music begins, and everyone who isn't seated quickly finds a place to sit. The minister, Pete, and Danny enter from the right side, turn and face the guests. Two precious children come down the center aisle slowly dropping lovely rose-colored hydrangea flowerets.

The bridal march begins. Rosie now comes into view as the guests' momentary gasps of approval are heard. She descends the steps, to be met by Connie. As the friends intertwine arms, Connie says, "Are you ready for this, Rosie, my friend?"

"I certainly am."

Rosie makes immediate eye contact with Pete and never varies her gaze. Pete's breathing quickens at her appearance and continues at the thought of his bride, soon to become his wife.

There isn't a whisper to be heard from the crowd, now standing in honor of this occasion. The blessed union, ordained by God between this man and woman, who are now ready to proclaim their everlasting love.

The ceremony is everything a couple hopes for as both pledge their undying love for each other. Tears are shed by many at the sheer beauty of the moment. Connie can't contain her elation, as tears of happiness for her friend are displayed unashamedly.

As the minister says, "I now pronounce you husband and wife; you may kiss the bride," tumultuous cheers, clapping, whistles and an errant catcall, greet the husband and wife as they, more than momentarily, show the deep love being felt by both through their elongated kiss.

The minister, while touching each on their shoulders, turning them toward the over exuberant guests, says, "May I present to you, Mr. and Mrs. Peter Roseman!" Yes, Rosie was no longer red but officially rose to match the flushed color of her cheeks, flushed with excitement and utter disbelief of this one small moment in her life, a moment so unexpected but now cherished for all time to come.

As Connie steps forward to return Rosie's bridal bouquet, Rosie whispers, "Thank you for helping us celebrate this day. I…uh…Connie, oh Connie, I wish so much…"

Connie quickly gives her a kiss on her cheek, answers, "I know, Rosie. I understand what you're trying to say, and I appreciate your well wishes for me."

The food and dancing quickly follow with numerous hugs, kisses, handshakes that were so hearty, Pete's arm soon aches all the way to his shoulder. But not Rosie, she never tires of this moment, as she knows she will never tire of the memories of this day.

ROSIE ROSEMAN

"Connie, thought I would call before we board the plane. I'll be checking in on you every few days until we are back."

Connie, as she exhales a sigh, "How sweet, but no ma'am, you won't. This is your honeymoon, and there's only one of those, so don't you let me enter your mind. This is all for you now, Rosie Roseman and your man. So you spend your time letting him know how much he means to you. But Rosie?"

"Yes."

"If your thoughts do turn my way, I hope it is with a smile and a happy heart!"

CONSTANCE LOUISE SINCLAIR

The prototype has been a welcome distraction as the weeks have flown. I like having a purpose, makes the time go by, and I love going to bed in need of rest instead of going to bed, because of the time. Even though my finances have dramatically improved-thank you, Lord for taking care of me once more-I don't feel comfortable with trying to get the ranch fully running.

The prototype is out of production, and there are three being tested at our oil sites here in Canadian County. The French office has advised that the validation of the system will not take long, after data has been compiled and results proven, to start receiving orders. All three United States locations are having dyes cast to assure prompt delivery.

"Connie, just checking in. I thought I should call sooner but just wanted to make sure I wouldn't be doing so too quickly."

"Oh Doug, no problem. Good to hear from you. I'm keeping up with you and Magic through the race circuits. Sounds like Magic is continuing on his quest to show us how magnificent he is. However, we all knew that, didn't we? You're a great trainer, and Magic has responded to you at every turn. Thanks so much for being there for me and giving me release and Magic his safety. It was a difficult time, and I was in such pain over having to let Magic go."

"I'm just happy I was able to purchase Magic, Connie."

"How are you and Amanda doing? I prayed after I left California that all this wouldn't be a detriment to you two."

"I know, Connie." Doug says and then with a sigh, continues, "I guess the word I'm looking for is a letdown. We had just had that one night before you arrived and then this circle of overlapping lives just seemed to engulf us. Amanda is withdrawn, melancholy and forlorn."

"She has no one, Doug? No friends her age? Does anyone ever come by? Has she entertained friends?"

"I can't say for sure, Connie. I'm never near the house most of the time, and when I am, it's only in the evening and at the back area."

"That's no good. Loneliness is a sad partner for a friend. Isn't she still seeing Magic train?"

"She stopped coming to Magic's workouts for a while, and Magic responded by not giving his all. I spoke with her, and she finally realized this doesn't only concern us, but Magic was feeling the fallout, also. From the moment Magic stepped from the hauler to the exit ramp, turned and saw Amanda...well, I believe she filled a place in Magic's heart that was empty. I think Magic's relationship with you had left a void, an emptiness and Amanda has displaced that, because within a day of her return to cheering him on, he, once more, started to show heart. Those two have created quite a bond. I believe Magic feels Amanda and what she's going through, and he doesn't understand when she isn't there. Connie, if it was just that easy for all of us to have the innate heart that Magic displays for those important in his life."

"Yes, that's a lesson we probably should all adopt. I guess we both underestimated Magic's need for stability. I feel quite ashamed as I merely thought of myself."

"You shouldn't, and your emotions were to be expected. Your reaction was normal, as you had a lot to absorb and process."

"Doug, how exactly is Amanda having trouble? You know, I don't think I even know her age. That speaks volumes about me! She's a beautiful child that shouldn't be weighed down with things over which she had no control. None of this was of her doing, and she absolutely had no say in her parentage."

"That will take a lot of convincing to make her believe that. She's so ashamed of her reaction toward Charles, upon finding out he was her father. And Connie, guess how she found out?"

"How, tell me?"

"From her Mother as she lay on her death bed." He hears Connie's heavy sigh. "Connie, I'm so sorry. I shouldn't be putting any more on you."

"You're not. My heart is breaking for that child. I've never been a mother, but I've lost a mother."

Doug continues, "She also blames herself for all the terrible things she said to Charles, or Charlie as she calls him. JJ found Amanda seated on the front porch with a loaded shotgun in her lap. Amanda tells JJ a man came and practically broke into the house through the sunroom. JJ kept insisting she call Charles and sees if she was in any danger, as the man was inquiring as to the whereabouts of Charles. Amanda wouldn't tell him and forced him off the property using the shotgun as leverage.

"Oh, no!"

"Connie, the man, was Louis Ludlow."

Connie gasps, as she exclaims, "Oh my! I had no idea. How terrible, did he come back?"

"No, she thinks he was frightened away as a Los Angeles County Deputy stopped him after he sped away from the property. Amanda believes that deterred any idea of return, as his name was now known by law enforcement."

"That was a relief, at least."

After several weeks of JJ's insistence, she finally called to speak with Charles and found out he was hospitalized. Her guilt from their last conversation made a compelling case for JJ to come to Oklahoma and not only check on Charles, but also on Ludlow's intentions. Charles had already passed when JJ arrived."

"I'm so sorry she couldn't have found closure with Charles."

"I agree completely as her feelings weigh heavily on her heart. On top of that, she feels responsible for you and JJ, because she begged him to come to Oklahoma to check on Charles but she had no idea he was tracking Ludlow."

"Still, Doug, she's at fault in no way in this situation. But guilt can be powerful and especially if the guilt you feel is toward someone that's out of your reach physically through death."

"Connie, just pray this will pass quickly."

"I will, Doug. Please take care. Love and hugs, my friend."

"To you also, Connie."

After disconnecting from Doug, Connie checks the time as she walks to the end of the dining room and sees that the lights are still on at her neighbors', the section north. She quickly locates Geri's number in her contacts and dials. "Geri, sorry to call so late, but I wanted you to know I'm going to be out of town if you wouldn't mind keeping an eye on the place. Great, I'll call upon my return. Hugs."

THE BORDILLON RANCH

Connie decides not to call ahead after landing at LAX as she just can't justify the call. It is still early in the day so why is the highway so congested? The traffic is overwhelming until she's well out of the city. How do people do this day in and day out? *"Unreal"* was her only thought while driving during a couple of tense moments.

As Connie enters the drive and places the car in park, she exhales as she looks toward the house and covered porch. She sees no other vehicles, but they could all be at the stables. What to do? Guess, knock on the front, and then try the sunroom door. She doesn't even give a second thought to removing the keys from the ignition, as the ranch is as secure as the estate. She is hoping to use the front entrance to be as discreet at possible. It isn't as if she has planned any of this other than the need to speak with Amanda.

Exiting the car, she asks God, *"Please let Amanda be at the house and not the stables. And*

Lord, please let her show me grace, and give me the words I need to speak with her."

Before she has the car door fully shut, she sees Amanda on the porch and Connie looks up and says, "Thank you, Lord, you always take care of me!"

Amanda's expression is hard to read but, that doesn't deter Connie from displaying a smile and giving the child a quick hug while words pour out of her mouth, of which Connie isn't even certain.

Connie chuckles to herself as she thinks, *"That wasn't so bad because Amanda was more receptive to hugs than Rosie had been the first time, and look where we are now."*

With a renewed sense of worth, Connie continues with the non-stop chatter and walks directly into the living area. As she turns, she's thankful when Amanda follows and shuts the door.

"Mrs. Sinclair. I wasn't expecting you!"

"I know. Please forgive me for dropping in like this, but I am so grateful you are home."

"Are you here to see Doug? I'm so sorry. Please have a seat, Mrs. Sinclair."

Connie takes one of the large leather chairs and immediately feels lost because of the overwhelming size. "Please call me Connie."

"Very well, Connie, would you like me to call Doug for you?"

"No, that won't be necessary as I've come to visit with you. I felt like we needed some girl time together." Connie, upon further thought, adds, "Only if that would be okay with you Amanda. I certainly don't want to push myself on you."

Amanda, slow to respond, looks into the kitchen area suddenly giving Connie the feeling she may not be alone. Then Connie silently prays, *"Oh Lord, please not JJ. I'm not ready. Please Lord."*

Amanda, still standing, says, "I'll fix us something. You must be hungry if you have just come from the airport."

Connie thinks that undeniably will break the ice. Food is always good, and she replies, "Thanks so much. That would be all right, but please don't go to any trouble."

Amanda says, "No trouble at all."

Connie jumps up and quickly follows Amanda into the kitchen. "I'll help if you don't mind?"

Amanda opens the cabinet, removes bread and two plates, and places them on the long granite bar as she flips on the lights. She then stands to look in the refrigerator and says, "Will ham and cheese be to your liking?"

"Perfect."

"Mayo or mustard?"

Connie replies, "Mayo."

Amanda chuckles, "Me too. Cheddar or American?"

"American, please."

"Me, too."

Amanda further queries, "Lemonade or Tea?"

"Tea for me," answers Connie as she anxiously awaits Amanda's reply, but none is forthcoming as Amanda pours one tea, one lemonade. Connie smiles; *two out of three isn't so bad. This might go okay.*

Connie waits to see if they will sit at the round table but Amanda places the plates on the bar after laying two placemats with napkins. Connie, to herself, *"Oh Lord, I would love your blessings over this food, but I'm in Amanda's domain at this time, so I'll say a quick, silent blessing."*

They sit in silence for a couple of bites, then Connie forges ahead, "I was thrilled to see in the racing results Magic is doing quite well." Connie states while trying to stay on common ground.

"Yes, he is. Magic is such a lover, and I try to take every opportunity to be wherever he's racing and even at his training trials. Magic has given me a purpose that I'd never realized was missing from my life." Amanda continues, and Connie realizes the two of them are identically at the same place in their lives.

After Amanda completes her thought, Connie says, “Yes, it’s wonderful to fall into bed at night, welcoming a night’s rest instead of sleep always being evasive.”

Amanda turning toward her displaying a smile says, “Exactly. And much nicer in the morning to be able to enjoy coffee as you look forward to the day ahead.”

Connie chides, “Well, I bet Doug plays a little part in looking forward to your day, also.”

Amanda now blushes and says, “Yes, he’s very sweet, kind, and has been most supportive. He always seems to know what to say and what I need to hear and also appears to instinctively know when I need him just to sit with me.”

“That’s wonderful. Having a touchstone is so essential for a healthy lifestyle. That’s what I call people who are there for me. I have a small plaque that says, ‘Friends are Angels who lift us up when our own wings have trouble remembering how to fly.’ I call them touchstones.”

Amanda while tilting her head, “I’ll have to remember that. That sounds lovely. Would you like cookies? I made them just yesterday. I have two kinds, oatmeal raisin and chocolate chip."

Connie smiles, thinking, *"Wow she bakes! She can show me up there,"* as she answers, "Both my favorites, so one of each please."

Amanda chimes in, "Mine, too. I'll get the cookies if you want to grab some glasses and milk. You do want milk, don't you?"

"You betcha." There's no way Connie was not going to drink milk, even if she choked.

In the other room, the conversation flows freely as the two sit facing each other leaning at opposite ends of the couch, with throws over their bare feet.

Evening approaches and as Amanda starts a fire, she says, "Your things in the car?"

Connie's mind races. She had forgotten to look for hotels on the drive up as her mind was on all the traffic.

Amanda drops the last log on the grate and turns as she realizes the reason for Connie's hesitance. "Uncle JJ isn't here if that's what's concerning you, and I want you to stay. Please say you will."

Connie feels relief, as she's thankful for Amanda's perception. They head for the car and upon opening the door, see a package that has been delivered. Amanda grabs it and tosses the parcel into the entryway.

The girls drag her luggage as Connie thinks, *"I brought an inordinate amount of clothes!"* But she smiles as she realizes, one whole case is full of shoes. *"A girl can never have too many shoes!"*

Connie struggles over the threshold and tosses her purse on the sofa where her purse quickly falls in a somersault fashion, making a perfect ten upon landing, but then falls forward as her mints roll out with several loose coins following.

Amanda says, "This way," making Connie's decision as to laying her stuff down and retrieving her purse items or continuing, moot.

Connie is impressed with the house as Amanda well notices. "After you unpack, I'll be glad to show you the rest of the house, but for now," as she enters the bedroom and opens the spacious walk-in closets which mirror each other making a small hall into the full spa bath, says, "I'll help you get settled."

"That's wonderful, Amanda. "You're more than a gracious host, and thank you for welcoming me into your home."

Connie notices as Amanda places some items in the closet that she's taking an unusual amount of time. "You like that?"

Amanda blushes and quickly places the blouse on the hanger and returns for another item.

Connie touching her arm, asks, "Amanda what's wrong?"

As their eyes make contact Amanda says, "I'll be back."

Connie moves a couple of steps to her right to free the way for Amanda to exit as she wonders, *what in the world, b*ut says, "Thank you for having me, Amanda."

Amanda leaves and while closing the bedroom door, says, "My pleasure. See you in a few."

Connie falls backward on the pillow-covered bed and watches as the fan slowly makes its journey around the ceiling. "Thank you, Lord, for Amanda's grace to me."

She rolls onto her stomach and making her way to the large expanse of windows in the second story bedroom, immediately notices how terribly dark it is. At home, she easily would be able to see the lights of the city in the distance; the pool would be illuminated, as well as the stables, not to mention the Wilson's lights living the next section north. *"Wow, how much land is here?"*

Shaking her head, she continues her task of unpacking and heads back to the living room as Amanda has not returned. Amanda has righted her purse, which is now on the leather ottoman with mints, a lip-gloss, and coins by it.

"Thank you, Amanda," as Connie drops the items in the bottom of her purse. "You know I used to call this my hospital purse as I'd ran into the Coach Store and bought the biggest bag that could accommodate my Ipad, journal, snacks, makeup and a few personal items. I never knew how long I was staying, so I tried to be prepared. Do you journal, Amanda?"

"No. I guess I never thought of journaling. Is journaling the same as keeping a diary? I'm familiar with that!

"You could say the two are related. I think of a diary as a once a day thing and mostly before going to bed. I journal when my mind has nowhere else to go but around in circles. I sat several nights at Charles' bedside and talked to him. My thoughts concerned nothing more than a realization that he and I were alive. The doctors said they were confident Charles could hear and identify my voice even though he was non-responsive. Sooner or later, my chatter would turn to silence with only the rheumatic sound of the respirator and my own breathing for company. I used my journal to dispose of things I couldn't express out loud."

"Like what?" Amanda asks with a puzzled look on her face.

"Oh, nothing like what you are thinking. Words that would just be negative thoughts. Things like, how this could have happened to Charles and me? Charles, what were you doing? Who was with you? Things that Charles didn't need to hear. There are things you can think to yourself but need to get out, so my journal fills that need." Placing her journal back in her bag, she continues, "But now, I call my purse my travel bag as it holds the same items but for a different purpose."

"I never carry a purse. I have a small wallet that holds everything I seem to need."

"Well, if that works for you, that's all that's important."

Amanda walks to the entryway and grabs the UPS package. Upon her return, Connie moves her purse to the floor, so that Amanda could have a place for the box.

Connie smiling, says, "Oh, I love receiving packages."

Amanda, still standing, says, "This is what I wanted you to see," as she pulls a pair of scissors from the desk drawer.

Connie's heart races a little as she's wondering, "What in the world?" She quickly scrunches to the edge of the sofa and notices the return address is Amazon. "You have me intrigued!"

Amanda continues her mission and lifts seven or eight plastic enclosed items, which Connie quickly identifies as clothing. Each so compact that they look as if they will self-inflate upon opening.

Connie, not knowing how to react, waits for Amanda to take the lead as this ball is definitely in her court.

Amanda tosses the box to the side and drops the still packaged items to the ottoman making a thump as they slide to an almost perfect semi-circle.

Connie, still waiting, gives up and takes control by saying, "Well. Let's see what we have here."

Amanda in a half disgusted and half-mournful voice while dropping in a slump to the sofa, says, "Don't you see? This is how I shop."

Connie, relieved the mystery has been solved, not to mention, that the "problem" is an area in which she's well-experienced, chuckles. Then she thinks, *"I'm even considered by many as a pro,"* pulls the girl to her and says, "This is something that can be easily handled but will be to the detriment of the poor UPS man." Connie gives a hearty laugh as she continues to hold Amanda in her embrace.

Amanda finally begins to see the humor of the situation, breaks into a broad smile as she says, "Really!"

Connie states, "Child, I'm a shopping pro, and when I'm on a mission, I've been described as a bird dog on point when I spy my item."

Connie with one fell swoop forces the sterile plastic enclosures to be thrown to the far side of the room.

"Tell you what, Missy Amanda." Both women, now sitting erect and facing each other. "Tomorrow you will dress from my closet, and then we hit the road for a marathon day of shopping."

Pure delight is seen in Amanda's eyes.

The following days turn into a week of fun as they have facials, massages, manis and pedis while the seemingly endless shopping continues. Oh and the shoes! Boxes and boxes of shoes, not only for Amanda but Connie, as her philosophy is if you like them, you need one in every color.

Doug is the first to notice the transformation when they attend Magic's workout. He has wondered what Amanda and Connie could find to talk over for this length of time and feels foolish for having a twinge of concern. He also is missing his time with Amanda and is a little tentative with Connie's encroachment.

"What do you ladies have scheduled for tomorrow?"

Amanda answers, "Depends on you and whatever Magic has planned."

"Well, that's easy then, as we have the day off." Doug blissfully answers and hopes he will be included in a little "Amanda" time, but his jubilance is short lived.

"Wonderful, I can use a down day, and I want to go through my new things. What do you think, Connie?"

"I'm all in for that. A girl's day home!"

The morning finds both women sleeping past their usual time with Amanda the first to rise.

Connie enters the kitchen, grabs a mug and heads for coffee as she glances out to the sunroom where Amanda is well settled on the settee. After pouring, Connie places her coffee to the side, as she notices a few coins and the initialed coin with the C for Charles, beside the pot. *How did the initialed coin come to be on the counter as it had been in the bottom of my purse?* The coin had been placed there when she was given Charles' things from the hospital and instead of putting his money in the plastic container for her to take, they handed them to her in an envelope, which contained bills, change, and the initialed coin.

Connie feels Amanda at her side as she reaches for her coffee and calmly states, "I was just headed your way. It looks like a beautiful morning just to relax."

Amanda says, "I found the money and coin under the edge of the ottoman. I believe they fell from your purse the first evening you were here."

"I'm certain you're right." Connie chuckles. She begins to scoop the coins toward the edge of the counter but stops abruptly at the feel of Amanda's grasp on her forearm.

Connie steps back and faces Amanda as Amanda places an identically initialed coin beside the one on the counter. Connie, at that exact moment, chills, as she feels Charles' presence.

Amanda's shoulders begin to shudder as she breaks into heavy sobs. Connie embraces her as she wonders, *"Is this the feeling of a mother's love for her child who is in pain?"* Connie unashamedly cries for the loss of a child to which she has never had the privilege of giving life.

DOUGLAS HARTLY

Doug walks toward the house from the stables like a man with a purpose and that's exactly what he is! He is intentionally going to crash their "girls' day." Enough is enough. He is going to be included at least for a cup of coffee or know why not!

With a short tap on the sunroom door, he lets himself in as he forcefully marches into the kitchen but stops short.

"What is going on?" he thinks as he turns on his heels and exits without even commenting. His once determined walk to the house is in full retreat to the solitude, not to mention safety, of the stables where, thankfully his only companion will be Magic. They are welcome to their "girls' day" if tears are involved!

"Sweetheart, come on. Let's find some tissue. Now tell me, what's wrong?"

"It's just, just, that coin. When I found the coin this morning, I didn't think anything about it until I sat down. Then after I thought, I jumped and ran to Momma's room."

Connie thinks, *"That must explain the one room Amanda failed to enter as I was being shown the house. Thank you, Lord, I was never curious enough to look for myself."*

"I started looking through her jewelry, and there it was. The coin I remembered seeing when I was smaller, and Momma let me play dress up. The coin is Charlie's, isn't it?"

"Yes," Connie says as she tries to find words. "So the coin makes you feel sad?" No answer from Amanda. "Or Amanda, does the coin make you mad? Mad enough to cry?" Connie's voice escalates with these words as she thinks, *"What am I doing?" Where am I going with this?*

Amanda finally opens up and says, "I guess a little of both. I'm sad because of what I said the last time I saw him, and I'm mad at Charlie because he died."

With that statement from Amanda, Connie realizes that's exactly what she had gone through. Sad because Charles was dead, but mad because of the circumstances in which he had left her. Almost destitute.

"Listen to me, Amanda. Listen carefully. Are you ready to comprehend what I'm going to tell you?"

Amanda, while reaching for a tissue, states, "I guess."

"What you're feeling is normal and natural, as I went through the same thing and yes, even journaled my feelings. I was sad Charles was gone, but at the same time angry at him for going. I cried and even screamed at Charles and God for what I was going through."

Amanda says, "You yelled at God?"

"Do you know Jesus, baby? He's a great comfort if you will let him into your life. I'll let you in on a little secret: our God is a big God and can take us being angry and hurt, because I guarantee you, He's sad right along with us."

"Let's make a deal, Amanda. Are you ready?"

Amanda as she captures a tear answers, "Okay."

"I'll tell you something concerning my husband you probably don't know, and you tell me something about your father, I probably don't know. Deal?" Connie feels relief at Amanda's non-reaction to the word "father" as she continues, "And when we are through, I'll give you a journal, and you can write all the things you need to leave on paper and out of your mind."

DOUGLAS HARTLY

Doug looks over his shoulder to make sure no one is the wiser as he, once again, places the binoculars to his eyes and continues his stakeout of the two in the sunroom. As he leans back from the window, he states aloud, "What the heck is going on? Oh man, they are passing the tissue box again."

AMANDA BORDILLON

"Are you hungry?" Amanda asks while heading to the kitchen, "Look at the time. No wonder I'm starved."

Connie laughs. "Let's see. Only the middle of the afternoon and still in our gown tails. I'm not telling if you're not. I'm going to pull on some pants and a tee but not going to guarantee a bra. Still early, right?"

"Okay, no bra, but I'm brushing my teeth," added Amanda.

Both head out as they look over their shoulders to see several haulers headed toward the stables.

"Wonder who that is?" Amanda states. "Hurry up, Connie. I'm starved!"

Connie already at the top of the landing says, "Want to know what you can do for me?"

Amanda as she joins her at the top, says, “What do you need? Anything, if I can?”

“Would you, could you, even though I’ve been told I don’t take instruction well. Could you teach me to cook?”

“You don’t know how to cook? Really?”

They shove each other as they head to opposite ends of the hall.

Connie shuts her bedroom door and checks her phone that she has left on silent from last night. After a deep breath, she sees two calls from the same number. She knows her time is growing short.

"Doug, the driver, just called and said they are just pulling back to the stables."

"Yes, I see them now."

JJ adds, "You did get everything I told you to procure?"

"Yes, everything."

"Did you check the website?"

"Yes, but I'm withholding judgment until I see the condition of what is in these haulers."

JJ chuckles as he adds, "Have a little faith in me, Doug ole boy."

CONSTANCE LOUISE SINCLAIR

"Sorry, I haven't returned your calls earlier. I'm visiting friends, a family in California. How soon do I need to be there?"

DOUGLAS HARTLY

"JJ, the girls. I don't know what's going on. They've been together for weeks and…"

JJ with concern in his voice, "And what, Doug...tell me!"

"JJ, don't be concerned. I think this is just girl stuff, but the last few days, there's been a lot of…of tissue passing."

"I'm on my way. I'll try and speak with Amanda in the meantime."

AMANDA BORDILLON

"Uncle JJ, where have you been? No, everything's okay. Oh JJ, things are better than okay. Connie is here and… and, well we have…oh, I don't know what to say. We have been shopping and talking. I've gotten clothes and shoes. A lot of shoes. I think I've broken my relationship with Amazon. But Connie said this would be to the detriment of the UPS man." Both Amanda and JJ laugh.

"What a relief. Both of them seem to have bonded."

Heading toward his truck, as the haulers have just left with their last load, JJ ponders, *"Where does this leave me?"*

"I think I'm catching on. What do you say, Professor?"

"I must admit this egg has no ruffles, and the yolk is still coddled in its appropriate position. The 7Up biscuits are light and fluffy and never fail to be flaky and tender. Hash browns are golden, and gravy is without a lump. Let's eat!"

"Amanda, after we eat, let's go to the barn, and see what all the commotion has been."

"I spoke with Doug, and its ponies and lots of them."

Connie's eyes light up as she replies, "I can't wait. Wonder if we can ride today? I've almost forgotten what riding feels like."

"I hope we can ride, too. I know we have plenty of tack and saddles."

DOUGLAS HARTLY

Amanda walks toward Doug and eagerly touches his arm. Upon turning, he states, "Well, hello, ladies. You finally decided to join the real world?"

Everyone chuckles as Amanda longingly looks at Doug. *"I've missed you. Really missed you,"* she thinks.

Connie says, "Where are the ponies? We want to see them!"

Doug, with a wide grin, points to the Gator and says, "Hop in and I'll show you."

They all pile in and head to the pasture. Upon topping a small incline, the girls gasp, and Amanda grabs Connie's arm.

"Ladies, say hello to the Mustangs!"

They sit speechless for a few moments, each in awe.

Connie is the first to speak. "Is there anything as beautiful as this? The sheer beauty of horses in motion, thank you, Lord, for these magnificent animals."

Amanda, speaking to Doug, "Where did we get them? Do we have enough pasture available? Oh look, one mare is pregnant. There's another. Have they all been vet checked and have all their health clearances? What do we need to do?"

Doug, in an all-out laugh, trying to decide which question to start with first, states, "Yes, to health. Yes to pasture, and don't worry, there's plenty we need to do."

"Where did we get them?" Then in a more conservative voice, "How much did they cost?"

Connie still absorbing their sheer beauty, thinks, *"What a good question!"* She feels a little pride stir in her chest at Amanda's cost concerns. She has a good head on her. Such an anomaly in one person. Most of the time, sweet child-like personification, but now the adult business side that everyone needs to have to be successful in life, morphs to the surface.

The business side I never had to be concerned with at Amanda's age has now been forced upon me. I will continue to be in control, and I pledge never to break weak. Yes, break weak was one of Charles' metaphors, but control feels well suited to me at this time of my life.

Doug continues, "These ponies are what JJ has been doing the last few weeks. You know he loves a purpose and especially if that purpose has anything to do with your happiness."

Amanda turns to face Doug, "My happiness?"

"Yes, he got the idea when you spoke of riding, and especially since Magic isn't a leisure option any longer."

"How far and wide did he have to search to obtain all these? He must have covered a lot of miles?"

"Well, yes and no. Most of this was handled online through the Bureau of Land Management.

The wild ponies and burros first received Federal protection in 1971, and the population then was estimated to be 25,000. The website was very informative and said the population has soared to 67,000 and along with that number, comes the cost. The cost is $49 million for their off-range care. You divide that amount between each pony, and that's $48,000 for one horse remaining in a corral over the horse's lifetime. Each year BLM only removes from the range the number of animals that can be adopted."

Connie silently listens, as they have slowly been moving with the band of horses so as not to lose sight. She likes the part concerning JJ doing whatever to insure the happiness of his family. *"He does have a good heart, Lord, doesn't he? Is this my first break-weak test? Can I balance it? Have a relationship while still being in control of my circumstances?*

Doug continues, "JJ has spent all his road time on obtaining transportation, and there has been an endless stream of supplies coming over the weeks. But for the rest of your questions as to cost, you can talk to JJ about that as he's headed home as we speak."

Connie realizes, and she thinks most gratefully, that she feels no need for flight at the mention of his return, even momentarily.

JJ enters and speaks to Miguel. "No one is at the house. Are they here?"

"No Señor. They are with the Mustangs and Señor Doug."

"Thanks, Miguel," JJ says as he hops in a Gator and has the four wheeler started and moving almost before the rest of his body can be pulled to safety. "Oh Lord, please let her be receptive."

The first two locations he checks is futile. Then, he thinks, *"It's still morning. Bet the ponies are at the pond, drinking."* He turns the gator and he considers, *"If that's their location, I've overshot them by a couple of miles."* The wind on his face feels almost cleansing, as JJ wonders what Connie is feeling. JJ's heart is ready to pound out of his chest at the anticipation of just seeing her once more.

Before he can even crest the hill, he pulls himself to a standing position while holding onto the windshield. The Gator coasts over the top before gaining downward momentum, and there they are. All three are standing at the edge of the pond, watching the Mustangs water on the opposite side. Amanda and Doug are hand in hand and Connie is to their right a few feet ahead. JJ pauses as the power of the moment overtakes him, and his eyes grow moist.

Upon hearing JJ applying the gas, the trio turns toward him, and then as they recognize him, Doug and Amanda immediately start his direction, waving their greeting. JJ's eyes are glued to Connie, as she's still as stone. Has she not recognized him or has she recognized him but feels no response toward him? Just as hope is seeping from JJ's soul, she heads forward and raises her hand.

JJ leaps from the Gator and first greets Amanda with a bear hug and a twirl and then shakes Doug's hand so aggressively, it catches him off guard. Connie, still a few feet back, slows her pace, but this does not deter JJ from turning his full attention her way and sweeping her off her feet in the identical greeting he has graced upon Amanda.

Connie feels a release….her heart, mind, and soul slowly shift from the endless circles so familiar to her. The circles of fear, the circles of feeling vulnerable, the circles of being used by men, the circles of being in love one moment and then the next being lost in darkness. Have these last few weeks brought them to a place where their lives could, ever so slowly, begin to blend?

Has she reached that place yet? Why hasn't she been able to allow herself to have happiness? It seems everyone else is happy. Rosie and Pete, Doug and Amanda, even Magic is well settled.

Connie hears all the platitudes she had journaled repeated in her mind. There's a small window on most things in life, and love is no different. Let go, embrace, with your whole body and soul what your heart so desperately wants and needs, a love that is here and so freely being offered to you before love finds someone else.

Connie hears the sound of distant thunder, and her body shivers with the all too familiar foreboding. At the same moment, JJ softly whispers, "Please Connie, can't you allow me another chance, please?" She opens her eyes as the two embrace, and she sees over his shoulder, in the distance, the dark clouds lifting and now revealing a rainbow with all the hope and promise of God's mercy, grace and peace!!!

Please join us in the sequel to "**A Different Season**" expected in the fall of 2017 "**Mist of the Moment**".

About the Author

Carol Nichols

Carol's legal career began her senior year as a secretary for an El Reno Law firm. She worked for the Canadian County Sheriff's Office under four different administrations and finished her Oklahoma career with the District Attorney's Office.

In southern Illinois, she worked for a prominent defense attorney.

Carol, as a mystery/romance author is a member of Romance Writers of America, Creative Quills and currently featured as a new author on Oklahoma Writers website.

Carol resides in El Reno, Oklahoma with her Jack Russell Terrier, Patches.

Made in the USA
Columbia, SC
24 April 2023

15417939R00250